CW00687761

The Tizzra Tragedy

© 2021 Anthony Baldwin

ISBN 978-1-09838-051-9

eBook ISBN 978-1-09838-052-6

THE TIZZRA TRAGEDY

ANTHONY BALDWIN

CONTENTS

CHAPTER ONE

The men wearily followed the night's bright full moon. Dozens of fatigued and scarred dark legs shuffled across the hard-cratered ground as they passed familiar trees. Dread inhabited these soldiers, even though most looked forward to going home.

Heda, one of the fiercest generals in their army, walked away from the rest of the warriors, snapped his spear in half over his knee, and twisted the blunt end into the ground so that the blade stuck up in the air. He stared upward and began muttering a plea to the black sky with the assumption that his words would reach his disappointed ancestors. He felt a connection to the stars that he hadn't experienced before. Bright lights encompassed by darkness. A good metaphor for his soul.

Another general, Sidra, turned back to look at his soldiers, making sure none fled. From the corner of his eye, Sidra saw Heda and realized what he was about to do.

"Stop him! Restrain him!" Sidra yelled.

Only a few men cared enough to pay attention and gaze over at Heda. None bothered to try to stop him. When Sidra noticed this, he scrambled to Heda. But it was too late. Heda sprung into the air and landed on the blade of his spear, causing his warm blood to spray out on the insects and dirt below. When Sidra came closer to him, he noticed that the blade was stuck in Heda's chest. This miscalculation gave him more time to live and curse himself further for his mistakes.

"Death is not ready for you, Heda. You must know that your spirit is stronger than any blade!"

Sidra pulled Heda off his spear and laid him down on the ground. He tried to block the blood pouring out of the warrior with his hands.

"Finish me. I have already pleaded with my ancestors. They long for me to dwell with them, Sidra. Their arms are open. I can hear their whispers… such praises! Any umbrage they have will be feeble in comparison to our queen's. Send me to them and tell my wives I died in the battle," Heda begged as he panted for air.

"The guilt of hurting you would kill me also, but I fear it would take too long to finish me."

"Kill me, Sidra. It would be sound for me to die by a general's hand instead of some passing lions. There is a beauty in it. Would you leave me alive for the vultures to taste?"

"No. Reflect on *my* ancestors. My ancestors would not look upon me with favor if I were the one who destroyed you. I use my spear only for my enemies. You will never be that."

"Then pass me your blade and I shall do it myself!" Heda yelled as more blood ran out of his wound, coloring the fertile ground a shiny maroon.

"We shall carry you back home. You can be healed there."

"It does not bewilder me that you lack the courage to kill. You proved that during the battle."

Sidra perceived what Heda was doing. Giving voice to the unspoken attitude that he felt was contaminating the soldiers. Sidra knew that eventually this sort of conversation would take place between him and some of the men. He was determined not to let anger rule.

"If you do not clasp your tongue, I will slice it off with a blunt spear! Now, we will carry you home," Sidra told him as he looked around for the nearest soldier to pick up Heda.

"No… I will need my tongue. I will need it to tell the queen the vile things you said about her before we left for this battle! I will need it to tell the other men about how feebly you expected them to do in the battle! And I will need it to tell your wife about how you failed to safeguard her two sons—"

Even though he was determined not to be goaded into action, Sidra was also tired and hurting, with less patience than he'd ever had. In a rage, he picked up Heda's spear and planted it firmly into Heda's chest. The general stood over him as life and blood left the man. The spear rose and dropped as Heda's breathing ceased. Then he took the arm bracelet Heda had worn for the last five years.

"I will award it to your wives," Sidra told Heda's corpse.

The other men were now some distance from Sidra. They had no desire to watch another general die. Sidra had not only lost the battle in Egypt they were returning from, but he had also lost the respect of some of the soldiers. But these losses were small in comparison to losing his two sons in the battle. Still, the general felt some relief that the other warriors didn't see what transpired with Heda. He did not want them to get the same idea and plant their spears into the ground. Reasoning thus, Sidra didn't call for any of them to help bury or carry Heda's body. He would indeed be left for the vultures.

* * *

Going into the battle, the warriors carried many supplies: skins for their water, extra weapons, extra shields. On their return, they carried heaviness, regret, humiliation. No one else considered doing what Heda did, but most would have understood. Their scars were proof of humiliation, which they received in abundance in Egypt.

Sidra was determined, after Heda's death, to make sure the men walked back into their city with pride. He took Heda's arm ring and put it on his most badly wounded soldier. He diverted the men to a nearby stream and directed them to wash themselves and their clothes. All were to present their spears and blades for inspection. Any that were broken or not sharp were to be repaired, replaced, or abandoned. Sidra would lead a search for any stranded birds, preferably ostriches, for large feathers. (He knew that he could probably find some vultures by Heda's body but the thought of…) The general felt pride in the remaining soldiers, and he wanted the city and the queen to see that pride in their appearance.

As he was sharpening a spear he had a revelation. He could not walk back into the city looking so presentable. The accusations the queen would make about them would be unbearably humiliating. Who can go into a battle without getting scarred and injured? "It looks like you were on a sabbatical instead of a fight! Were your feathers not even ruffled? Where did you hide so that you should look so pristine?" Sidra feared that any pride he gave the men would be destroyed in the briefest of moments by the ignorant ramblings of the queen. In fact, the soldiers looked too polished to him now. They should have more scars to show the queen and the city to prove they did indeed suffer. Sidra explained this to the warriors. They understood. The feathers that were gathered were abandoned, spears broken in half, garments ripped. The general ordered all the men to sit in front of him, and with his blade he started to strategically cut the men. At first, he cut with hesitation and sympathy. But when one of the soldiers spoke up and stated, "General! It must look like war!" Sidra realized what he needed to do. He ordered the men to pull out their blades and slash each other's bodies. He told them to focus on the arms, legs, chest, and back. But not the face. He would administer those scars on select soldiers himself.

Restraint was evident in the warriors, though they understood the general's logic. Still, it took a lot for these warriors/ survivors to turn their blade on the same men to whom they owed their lives. Sidra realized this too, so he had half of the men face the other half.

"Those on my left, take your blade or spear and slice the left leg of the man in front of you," Sidra commanded. The men did as he said. "Now, those on my right, slash either the chest or arm of the man in front of you." They did so. As he gave these orders, he walked up to random warriors and he took his blade and made cuts on their faces or scalps. "Those on my left, slash either the backs or arms of those on the right until I am satisfied and tell you to stop." Again, his orders were followed.

Several minutes after everyone was bloodied, Sidra ordered that they stop and again visit the stream to clean off. Afterwards, they camped for a day and rested in the hot sun to let their wounds begin to heal, at least physically.

* * *

One day later, the men arrived in their city. Again, it was night, and the same feelings of shame and disgrace were running through the same weary men, except for Tizzra. Tizzra was the finest soldier in the land; this was unsurprising to most because his father, before he died, was the greatest soldier that the city had ever seen. His father was also a good friend to Sidra. Tizzra was nineteen years old and had been a soldier for more than two years. During their battle with the Egyptians, Tizzra had shown wisdom in his actions and was responsible for saving many of the remaining soldiers' lives. With the battle behind him, he only wanted one thing: a wife. He had long been in love with one of the queen's servants named Chara. Servants were rarely released for marriage, so Tizzra had doubts about there ever being a union between the two.

A guard saw the men approach the city's outer walls.

"The men have returned! They are back! Someone alert Khama!" The guard shouted as loud as he could while he ran to meet the soldiers. In his haste, he even forgot to grab his torch.

"Is this all of you? Did you prevail? Where are the others? Are there others?" he said as he glanced over the dirty, tired, still bleeding men, none of whom had any intention of answering his base questions. The guard looked at Sidra.

"Sidra breathes? Ha!" the guard muttered to himself.

"We must see Queen Azmera," Tizzra demanded.

"We were instructed that if you were to return after dusk or in the early morning, you must wait and meet her in the courtyard after dawn. The queen does not want to address soldiers in the dark."

Tizzra turned to the soldiers, "We are to meet at dawn in the queen's courtyard. Go home until then."

The men didn't want to disperse. Only a few cared to go home. Although they wanted to see their families again, they felt as if their fallen friends were looking on over their shoulders. Tizzra gently pushed a couple of soldiers, causing the rest to get moving. Sidra leaned against a wall and watched as the men set off tiredly toward their homes. The men. These were his men, and although they were still alive, he felt as if he had failed them more than the dead men he left in Egypt. "Why did I bring them back? I should have kept letting them get... if it was good enough for my sons..."

Tizzra shuffled over to him.

"What can I tell her? How can I proclaim?" Sidra said as he fought back that rare burning wet sensation growing in his eyes.

"She knows it was a slippery battle. As do most of the women in the land. They knew the reality of it as we marched out of the city, certainly more than we warriors. The women have had many days to mourn us. Your wife has been prepared, I am certain of it. But now she at least has you. Your words must be a blanket to her. She must be given every sort of comfort there is. You must weep with her; you must hold her and wipe her tears. And then you must give her solace and then pride. Declare that her sons fought bravely."

"And died needlessly. Oh, whose fate is worse: her ears to hear or my mouth to tell?!"

"Declare that our battle was tough... and there were so many of them. Your words must take her to the battle so that she will understand. Try to transform the horrors we saw into the words she will hear."

"Blame will fall on me! From the entire land! How could I carry Heda home? I carry enough already. I carry the blame and embarrassment of our loss. I carry the blood of all our dead friends. And I carry the responsibility of it all... alone."

Sidra waited for Tizzra to respond. He was desperate to hear that his old friend's son didn't nurture the same feelings that the other soldiers did. But Tizzra did not respond.

"Do you curse me too, Tizzra? Does your stomach clinch when you think of me? Certainly, this is true of the other men."

"No. It was a brutal battle, impossible to win. My shoulders grow broader when I think of you. You did well."

"So did you. Now, go. Go surprise your mother."

Tizzra ran off. Sidra relaxed against the wall for a moment recalling his sons' deaths. He had assured his wife that their sons would return even if he didn't. Everyone in the battle could bear witness that Sidra had done all that he could to protect his sons. He gave them the tamest responsibility during the battle, but it just wasn't enough to keep his sons alive. Azmera required all the generals to take their sons into battle with them because she believed it would boost the morale of the soldiers and motivate the generals to achieve victory. Sidra stopped dwelling on his sons when he noticed that some of the city's guards were staring at him. A few, he thought, were laughing. He walked away.

CHAPTER TWO

Tamrin was a sixteen-year-old orphan from Egypt. When he was four, his parents were killed by thieves, and he was brought to Nubia to be sold as a slave. When Sidra heard about this, he had the thieves killed and took Tamrin into his household and raised him. He didn't bother much with trying to make Tamrin feel like he was part of his family because he felt that no one else in the village would see him as such.

After leaving the guards, Sidra sat on a huge rock outside of Azmera's palace pondering what to tell his wife. His rumination was so intense he didn't notice Tamrin approach him.

"General! Yes! At last! The city will be refreshed like a rainstorm! No one greater has ever passed through our city walls! Praises go to your ancestors'! I did not expect to see you again!" Tamrin yelled, snapping Sidra out of his daze.

"Tamrin. My wife?"

"She is doing well although she has been filled with worry. How was the battle?"

"What sort of wicked humor causes people to keep asking that? Do you see me wearing any Egyptian clothing? Do you see their general's head pierced on a pole? Do you view a caravan of slaves? No. You do not view these things because we did not account for much in the battle!"

"Then you escaped? But how?"

Sidra gave no reply.

"I will ask your sons if you do not feel like talking. I should have been more thoughtful. Where are they?"

"They are dead. The Egyptians slaughtered them. I could not even take measures to bring their bodies back with me. Their spirits are captive in Egypt."

"They killed them? Those murderers! Imagine it! A land that deserves no rain or sun or joy presumes that it has the right to slay those greater than them!" Sidra's sons treated Tamrin like a brother whenever Sidra or his wife wasn't around.

"They are your people. You have the same blood."

"You disgrace me by calling them my people. You and your family are my people. This is the land my heart lusts for. I thirst to know which ones were responsible. My blade would show them no mercy."

"Is it so?"

Sidra stood up and started to walk away, but he paused and walked back to Tamrin.

"Tamrin, let us say that you had two sons. If I told your sons to fight with lions—when those lions killed your sons, whom would you regard as liable for their deaths?"

"The lions...and I suppose you also for telling them to fight the lions."

"That is what Azmera did. With the flick of her tongue, she sent us to clash with lions! She did it with half a thought. We should—"

Sidra arrested his tongue. Looking at Tamrin, he didn't see the young man who lived with him for twelve years; he saw another person who would soon lose respect for him.

"I must see my wife before rumors reach her first."

Sidra walked off. The thought of others talking to his wife first finally gave him the motivation he needed to see her. Tamrin hiked over to a large rock that was one hundred feet from the entrance of the city and sat on it. He rested there dreaming about what he thought Sidra was close to saying to him. He had a longing to be important like Sidra, but he thought the likelihood of that happening was small because he was not a Nubian. But now, even he could smell the opportunity in the air. With Sidra's sons dead, Tamrin believed that Sidra would be forced to accept him in a way that he hadn't before. He knew that something great was forthcoming, and he wanted a share of it.

"That stupid woman! She should have let me fight!" Tamrin muttered to himself as he sat on his rock. Azmera needed all the men she could get to fight in her battle, but she told Sidra that under no circumstances was Tamrin allowed to accompany him. Her reasoning being that she didn't want the Egyptian soldiers thinking he was a slave or that he, in any way, contributed to the success of her army. She pondered that they might look at Tamrin and think that he aided the soldiers with intelligence.

Azmera considered many scenarios about what she would do with Tamrin. She thought about parading him around and telling everyone that he and Egyptians like him were untrustworthy. That would not have worked because everyone who knew him knew that Tamrin was a decent young man.

Tamrin had dreamed for years about going into battle with Sidra, and when this opportunity came up, he was certain that he would, at last, get his chance. Sidra had filled his head with stories of war and skirmishes. He even trained him in warfare, Tamrin being more skillful at it than Sidra's sons. He longed to see Sidra handle himself in battle, and he wanted to show him how well he could handle himself. Now, Tamrin was hopeful about his evolving relationship with Sidra. "He must know that I would have fared better than his sons in the battle. This must upset him," Tamrin muttered to himself. Then he smiled as he thought about his future, which he believed was secure no matter who was ruler over the land, Nubian or Egyptian. He had ties to both.

* * *

Most of the huts in the village farthest from the queen's palace were in a valley. A long uneven wall made entirely of rocks and mud circled much of the village. The wall was three feet high at its zenith and only eighteen inches at its shortest. Children would put pebbles, sticks, and dirt in between the cracks of the rocks. In nearly every cubic meter in the wall, there were holes for holding long torches, and on certain nights these torches were set on fire to light the village. Torches were also placed sporadically throughout the village. Weary nomads appreciated seeing these flaming lights. Some animals feared them and stayed away from the village.

Tizzra's hut was on a hill outside of the village. He shared it with his mother. It was thirty feet in diameter and stood under a large acacia tree. His father built it there so that the shade would soothe his family in the middle of the blazing days. However, there were a lot of insects in the tree that found their way into the hut below. Sidra's hut was on the opposite side of the village. Tizzra ran so fast to see his mother that the flame from his torch almost singed him before he reached their hut. He stopped before he entered his home, dropped his torch on the ground, and kicked dirt on it to extinguish it. His heart was beating hard, partly because of his running but also because he knew that he was about to give his mother a great surprise that few mothers in the village would experience. He dropped his spear and shield at the entrance next to the smoldering torch and entered the hut.

"Wake up. Wake up, Mother!"

His mother woke up and paused, shocked, at the sight of him. When she realized that she wasn't dreaming, she rushed to embrace him. As she did, she thought that maybe the battle wasn't as bad as everyone thought it would be. Tizzra winced because of the barely healed wounds on his back and chest. She imagined that most, if not all, the soldiers were able to return home. *"Perhaps the battle did not even take place,"* she briefly thought.

"Tizzra! You endured!" his mother shrieked.

"With many wounds, as you can see. They fought us on chariots that were taller than I. And I have never seen horses so strong. Most of us were killed. Their numbers were like the grains of sand on the beach… ours were like the grains of sand in a little girl's hand."

"Who was killed?"

"All the generals save one, and most of their sons. Sidra's sons too. They were the first two attacked."

"By the ancestors, Tizzra! What did Queen Azmera say to you?"

"We have not seen her yet. We are supposed to go at dawn."

"Are you tired? Lie down. Go lie down."

Tizzra crawled over to a large bundle of feathers and laid his tired and bruised body down. Nubian mattresses consisted of leaves, dirt, or feathers covered with animal skin. Azmera encouraged everyone to sleep, not on the floor but on an elevated bed. She even sent Sidra and his soldiers on a mission to collect animal skin (preferably from zebras) to distribute to the villagers. Still, many of the older villagers preferred to sleep on the ground.

"Yes, I feel a heaviness for Sidra," Tizzra said as he closed his eyes to sleep.

"Was he killed before his sons were?"

"He was not killed. Although he may soon wish he was if he receives the chastisement everyone thinks the queen is going to give him." Tizzra changed the subject, "Have you seen Chara?"

"I spoke with her yesterday. She fares well. Now, sleep. I will wake you."

Tizzra's mother desperately wanted to ask him more about the battle, but she decided to let her son rest. She laid down and thought about Sidra returning to the city. It was unfavorable for a general to return home after losing a battle, but Sidra would make sure that he did, for his wife. The last serious battle that these Nubians had fought was two years before this failed attempt. Then she thought about Sidra losing his sons while she was able to keep hers. While Sidra's boys died an embarrassing, painful death, her son was not only alive, but he was full of life, hopeful about his future, dreaming about marriage.

The biggest hut in the village belonged to Sidra. It was near the rock gate that surrounded the village. Five torches were lit around his hut. This let him know that his wife was awake. Sidra went inside his home and saw women sitting on the ground crying with his wife, Oja. When their eyes met Sidra's, the crying stopped.

"Leave us," Sidra told the women.

They got up and walked out, still upset over the death of Sidra and Oja's sons.

"What did they tell you?" Sidra asked.

"My sons are dead?"

"They are. My feet have hurried to be with you, but I was delayed. You should hear the truth from me. Do not listen to what others are telling you, I was there! I tasted the wickedness that took place at the battle. I wear the scars!"

Oja didn't want to hear anything from Sidra. She had always believed that he cared more about his image and rank in the city than about his son's lives. But she had learned a long time ago not to talk too much when Sidra felt his pride being attacked.

"What else did those women tell you? What were they moaning about me?" Sidra asked.

"They only told me that you survived, and our sons were missing."

Before Sidra could respond arrogantly to his wife, he heard someone outside calling his name.

"Sidra! Sidra!" the voice said.

"Who is it?" Sidra yelled out to the voice.

"It is Khama. Come out." Sidra walked out immediately. Khama was Queen Azmera's advisor. He had served her faithfully for many years despite how he personally felt about her haughtiness and injustice. Sidra was certain that Khama was there to bring him bad news from the queen.

"Khama, what is it?"

Until Khama actually heard Sidra's voice, he didn't believe that the general was still alive. Rumors were stronger than facts in the villages, so Khama was justified in his doubts. When he saw Sidra standing in front of him, it made him wonder about the rumors he heard about his sons' deaths.

"Sidra. I was just awoken moments ago by one of the guards. My ears are yours."

"Our casualties were severe...in both men and supplies. About eighty men returned with me. There may be a few wounded who might show up later. And in the morning, we are supposed to see Azmera, to receive our reproof. Oh, a warrior's return!"

"I will talk to her before she sees you to try to calm her and reason with her. Although she normally detests reason. Just like she spits on wisdom, swats at mercy, and vomits on decency."

Khama turned and looked around for any eavesdroppers. When he didn't see any, he moved in close to Sidra.

"I will be with you in the morning. You will have my backing. I will remind her of your faithful service to our land. You will see what a true friend is in the morning. I will not let her question you without defending your valiant service," Khama whispered.

These were the words that Sidra desired. They were more satisfying to him than any banquet could ever be. He was used to people being on his side, something that had been declining from his life in the previous months. Khama had opened a vein that would allow Sidra's dissatisfaction to flow out. He gathered the courage to question the queen's actions in front of her main advisor.

"What induced her to do this? Even children knew this tragedy would befall us, and she sent us anyway," Sidra said as *he* looked around for eavesdroppers.

Both men were ready to let their dissatisfaction show freely. Khama had waited for months for anyone to express discontentment with the queen. Although the mood and circumstances were grim, Khama felt a bright spark of hope.

"This had to do with the king," Khama told him.

King Nospri had been dead for years. He was murdered while traveling back from Egypt. Everyone in the villages knew the story of how robbers killed Nospri and the members of his caravan and stole his jewels, including his "blue diamond," which was, in truth, just an odd-shaped, blue crystal that he kept because he took it out of a dead lion's mouth.

"She thinks the bandits who killed him were Egyptian?"

"I gather she does. I suspect so too. You were there. Did you never suspect it?"

Khama pulled on Sidra's arm and led him behind his hut to make sure that no one else was listening.

"I think it was over an Egyptian woman. He may have forgotten himself and gotten involved with a woman." Khama continued, "Do not tell anyone I said that to you. It may not be truth."

"Then my sons' blood dries on foreign soil because of her speculations," Sidra said. He was on the verge of tears again, tears that Khama did not want to see.

"Your wife requires her husband. Go and be with her. I will see you at the palace."

Khama picked up his torch and started walking to the west side of the village. Sidra stood outside to make his eyes stop crying. He didn't wipe his tears away because he felt that that would make more tears come. No, he believed if a Nubian man wanted to stop crying, the power to do so would have to come from within him. Once Sidra stopped himself, he went back inside to his wife.

"I heard what you said out there," Oja told him in a whisper. "You will see us dead also? Azmera held no position in Egypt; you did! And I see few scars on you! A protective father would be a mutilated father!"

Nubian women rarely challenged their husbands like Oja did unless they wanted to be hit or expelled from their home. But the thought of doing either didn't occur to Sidra. After Oja's comment, he wondered if he should have let the soldiers wound him more severely.

"I grieve my sons, woman. Have you no solace? You have *heard* about their deaths; I had to watch it occur!" Sidra inquired.

Oja stared at him for a moment. He had lost his sons, just like her. She knew that. But she also recalled that he promised to keep her sons alive. In Oja's mind, he was responsible for their deaths. Nevertheless, she took a deep breath and then put her arms around him.

An hour later, Sidra went outside and slashed himself further with his blade.

CHAPTER THREE

Very few of the warriors went directly home as they had been told. Although they all desperately wanted to see their families, they didn't want their families to see them covered in still bleeding wounds, reeking of defeat (which Nubians thought was a real scent), filled with sorrow over dead friends, brothers, sons, and fathers.

The warriors felt as if they were being sent back home as punishment from the Egyptians. A weird kind of reverse curse: Those who did not fight as well were killed in battle but lauded and honored at home. Those who fought better kept their lives but faced anger and disappointment from their families and queen. Adding to their concerns was the fact that there was a retreat called by a general.

Khama caught sight of a few of the warriors skulking around his village. With a concerned look on his face, he approached them, compassionately touching their shoulders.

"How many? How many returned?" Khama asked.

"Fewer than a hundred."

"So few? Such a brave few! The rest are dead? In Egypt?"

"Yes. But a few died on their way back home. They could not survive the journey."

"Gather all that you can and have them meet me outside the north village wall," Khama said as he turned away to walk to the wall.

The three soldiers who heard Khama wasted no time in doing what they were told, except they did not visit the few soldiers who were brave enough to already go to their homes. Many who were still hovering around the villages and city missed out on the meeting as well because the warriors were so eager to hear what Khama had to tell them that they didn't do a complete sweep for their comrades. No matter—they would tell them later.

At the north wall, Khama stood motionless as more and more soldiers arrived. Looking to the east, he pondered how long it would be until sunrise. Not wanting to wait anymore, he addressed the men.

"There has not been a moment of peace in the land since you men left. All my ears have heard has been your women and children crying. I have seen your farms overtaken with pests and birds and neglect. Your wives and babies have been hungry. Your homes, deteriorating. Your mothers wailing day and night. From this village, I could hear them all the way to the palace. They made that a certainty until they were ordered to stop. The queen gave that order so she could take slumber. Take slumber! Yes, while your wives, mothers, and children cried, she slept! No, she did not want them to show concern. You are warriors. If you will fight against a land that has not threatened you, I am sure you will fight against a woman who is destroying you. Have I misjudged any of you?"

They all stated, "No." Khama had stirred their anger. As they looked at each other, they saw nothing but vengefulness on each other's faces.

"Then I must ask you to go into battle again. And unlike your last one, this battle will have a blessed resolution. This kind of rulership cannot stand. A crazed jackal is sitting on the throne and curses will be on us if we let her stay there. Spread my words but be discreet. Tell none of your wives or families. Only your fellow soldiers or those you know will be with us. These are strong ideas that must only be kept between strong ears. My plans are young. As they mature, you will hear. Remember our hope while you are at the palace in the morning. Now, finally, go home until the assembly. Look upon your children. Give them a future!"

More hopeful, the men dispersed a second time. Khama pondered what he would say to Sidra to lure him to his side as he made his way back to the palace. In his mind, Khama dared Sidra to refuse his suggestions. *'The man loves to follow orders— let him follow mine. The man loves to fight—let him fight for my cause. If he can be a pet willing to sacrifice his own children, then he can sacrifice for me.'*

The entire city waited in the courtyard in front of Azmera's palace for several hours for their queen to appear. The queen's courtyard was close to two hundred yards in diameter and was surrounded by torches placed five cubits apart from each other. During the night, the guards always made sure that at least two of the torches were always burning. The tile on the floor was made of large mud bricks that were dyed different colors (red, blue, and black) depending on the location. Most of the crowd, though, had to stand on the sand behind the tiled area, and even more had to stand on the dirt or grass beyond that.

The heat blazed down on all the villagers so intensely that it felt as if the sun had been smeared on their bodies. In this kind of heat, a cool breeze was as valuable as an ounce of gold. Queen Azmera's position in the courtyard was under a big Argoun palm tree, so she would typically speak for long periods of time without concern for the hot villagers. Her advisors had learned a long time ago not to bother telling her that the people were getting tired; she didn't care about that. However, when they told her that it was time for her to eat, she would dismiss her subjects.

Like nearly everyone else in the courtyard, Sidra and Tizzra were deep in conversation. Sidra subtly dropped in suspicions about Queen Azmera. Tizzra noticed them and then gazed around to make sure that no one else was listening in on their conversation. He got very uneasy when Sidra confessed that he had planned to avoid the battle altogether by running to a foreign land the night before they were to go into battle.

Sidra's words frightened Tizzra, so he fabricated an excuse and walked away. He investigated the crowd of villagers and noticed his closest friend, Kito. Kito was five years older than Tizzra, and he used to want to be a soldier, but his right hand was practically useless to him after an attack. He believed that he had taken all the pain his body was supposed to handle, so now he spent most of his time with his wife and children. To deal with the pain, he would stay drunk from wine. Kito and Tizzra walked toward each other.

"Tizzra, out of the thousands of rumors moving through the city, it seems like the only true thing that I heard was that Sidra was still alive," Kito said.

"Yes. It was a gruesome battle. So many were killed. So many of us, I mean," Tizzra replied.

"Is it true that you withdrew to a river? Is it true that Sidra declared a retreat?"

"My friend, you were not there. And no one who was absent can see the story clearly. Not even the circling birds that flew above us in Egypt or the numerous ants on the battlefield. Only the soldiers can grasp what took place. So, please, do not judge the general too harshly. We take choices for granted; Sidra did not have any. They were a strong army with better weapons than ours. He fought more bravely and ferociously than the other generals. And if we had not retreated, everyone, including me, would have died fighting."

"I do not judge him. That is Azmera's delight. She will conclude that he is a coward since he is the only general left alive. She will think he hid himself while the others fought. I passed by him... I did not see too many scars or wounds on him... not like you."

Tizzra didn't like hearing people talk about Sidra any more than he liked hearing bad things about the queen. He was happy to see his friend but disinclined to hear his lack of sympathy for Sidra. Despite this, he continued talking to him.

"Perhaps we soldiers will attack Azmera's ears with the knowledge of what occurred." Tizzra changed the subject from Sidra. "Have you seen Chara lately?"

"No." Kito changed the subject back. "Did Sidra truly command a retreat, or did you soldiers do it yourselves?"

"He bid it." Tizzra again changed the subject. "I intend on asking Azmera to grant Chara to marry me. Do you think she will approve it?" Tizzra asked.

Chara served in the queen's palace along with several other women. When the soldiers were ordered to do repair work on Azmera's palace, her servants would bring the men water to drink. That is how the two met. She was tall and beautiful. Any man in the village would have been glad to have her for a wife (or a second wife).

"My friend, it is unlikely. She has only released a servant once. She keeps a firm hold on her servants the way a poor man would grip a sliver of gold. And a good woman like Chara… any queen would want to keep," Kito said.

"On our way back from Egypt, she was all that I could think of. Every thought of mine embraced her. I could not even properly dwell on those who perished. She pushed those sad, morose thoughts out of my mind," Tizzra told Kito as he noticed Azmera, her female servants, and her advisor walk to the palace courtyard. When the villagers saw the queen, they immediately became quiet, moved to their correct locations, and gave their attention to her.

Azmera walked to her seat underneath her tree. When she sat down, a refreshing cool breeze came through the courtyard, which she took to be a sign of approval from her ancestors. She tossed her hand slightly into the air, signaling for one of her servants to bring her some water. After the queen drank it, she stood up to address the crowd.

Also taking their pre-assigned places were the *mundutu*. These were men who would stand on portable tree stumps that were placed in strategic spots in the crowd. They would repeat as loud as they could the words of the king or queen so that all in the crowd could hear what was said. Nospri decreed that everything that was said at an assembly be repeated for everyone to hear. That way, if he were addressing a soldier or general, the entire conversation would make sense to the audience. After he died, Azmera only wanted what she said repeated to the crowd, even though she knew that sometimes when she was talking to someone else it didn't make sense to the audience.

There were eleven *mundutu*, and they were mostly elderly men who otherwise would have been sent to Egypt to fight with Sidra. Naturally, they were all very loud men, but because of their age they found it difficult to stand for as long as Azmera spoke. Khama had recently suggested that they be replaced by loud women. Azmera considered it but decided against it because she wanted the only feminine voice heard to be hers. As the *mundutu* took their positions, a couple of the men had to be helped onto their tree stumps, which were also very old. The men refused to replace them because the stumps had supported them on many significant declarations that took place in the city, including the king's death.

"We lost the battle against the Egyptians! In a moment, we will discern why. But first, let me express that there are battles and there are wars. And we will languish through both if we must! Why? It is because they plot to steal our land from us. They plot to dismantle our dignity and take us as their slaves. They are conquerors of the fragile! Do not miscalculate them, they have accomplished it before. Woe to those who cannot see that they want to creep into our land and snatch it from us! Destroy our gods and carry us off in their mouths to be their slaves! Their hearts are itching to see you as dusty slaves bereft of culture or tradition. They will esteem you so lightly that they will not even enlighten you as to theirs. Their swords are damp with the blood of villagers who underestimated them in the past. What would you think of me if I did not want to shield you? Wisdom forced me to assail them first with our best men. Now, general, confess to everyone... what happened to our best men?" the queen said as the thousands in assembly turned to look at Sidra, who stood next to his soldiers amassed to the left of Azmera.

"The men were killed, Queen Azmera," Sidra told her. The queen motioned for Sidra to come forward.

"Show the crowd your face," she told him.

Sidra slowly turned to the crowd after he walked up to the queen. He tried to look at the distant horizon, but his eyes met those of his wife, which made him comfortable enough to keep his head up. Oja stood next to her two friends, both widows who had lost their husbands in the same skirmish that Tizzra's father died in. In their hearts, they blamed Sidra because he refused to give out any details of their husbands' deaths.

"Why were our men killed?" Azmera asked with an intense look in her eyes, the muscles in her brow clenched as hard as she could get them. She made all her movements and expressions as grand as she could to pull attention toward herself.

"It was a victory that we could not have tasted. There were—"

"'A victory we could not have tasted'?! Such an appalling stance for a general!"

Many in the crowd became discomforted. Sidra looked away from his wife and tried to notice everyone who was murmuring against him. Azmera grew tired of staring at the back of Sidra, so she got up and walked to him, breaking precedent.

"Reveal to us what transpired! There are countless widows and orphans who want to know what occurred! You dare to pressure me to pry it out of you?!" the queen told him.

"Possibly... I surmise that we were spotted by spies a day before the fight. They appeared to have insight into our skills and numbers. During the battle, many men were run through; others were run over by their chariots. We were studied."

"I bestowed you with gifts to ensure that you would not be harmed. What happened to them?"

"They were seized before the battle."

Azmera gave Sidra four white cats to take into battle with him. She had heard about the Persians who went into battle against the Egyptians and put cats on the front line. The Egyptians believed that cats were sacred, so they didn't attack for fear of hurting one of the felines. The Persians won the battle.

Unfortunately, it didn't work out that way for Sidra and his men. He had given the cats to his two sons to make sure they wouldn't be attacked. However, the Egyptian general in charge of the fight did not believe in the sacredness of felines, so he ordered twenty of his men to surround both of Sidra's sons. Then he climbed down from his chariot, pulled his sword from his sheath, and slashed the necks of Sidra's two scared sons. The cats dropped to the ground, and two of the Egyptian soldiers picked them up, put them on their chariots, and rode off, away from the battle area.

"Those glorious animals were captured? No Nubian general has had such an advantage! Then what happened?" Azmera asked.

"A pitiful, relentless struggle. We were being slaughtered swiftly, so, to live, I ordered a retreat to a nearby river. It was near night."

The response that breezed through the crowd was no surprise to Sidra. No general had ever ordered a retreat. It was unthinkable! Men would run away from a battle, but they would do so of their own initiative, not by a general's order. So, when the people heard this, there was unease throughout the assembly.

The fact that any men returned at all would suggest that a retreat took place. However, for these Nubians, there were situations that allowed soldiers to return without a retreat being declared. If the second or third wave of warriors were being defeated, typically the other warriors would not engage in the battle but would disperse from the battlefield without uttering a word to each other until that night. Also, while losing a battle, a general could make an appeal to an opposing general to call an end to the battle, to admit a loss. Third, if enough warriors agreed to it by their actions and by their words, they could cause a retreat. But not a general. Under no circumstances would the men hear their general utter the words. Under this third scenario, the soldiers were to forcibly remove the generals from the battlefield so they could keep their honor and dignity.

For Sidra, none of these options were feasible, for they were fighting a different foe than they were accustomed to. The Egyptians showed no intention of anything less than annihilating their enemy. So there would be no appeal to end the battle. As quickly as Sidra could turn his head, he saw father or son being slaughtered before anyone else could yell "retreat!" His spear was useless, but his tongue was not. Therefore, the general used his only weapon to save the lives of those who remained.

"You proclaimed a retreat?" the queen asked as she walked around Sidra to create a dramatic effect for the audience. Her eyebrows tensed a little bit further, and she stared at him with a stare of disbelief, even though Khama had already told her about the retreat hours earlier. Some of the surviving soldiers began to grimace with disgust when they heard the disrespectful tone Azmera spoke to Sidra. However, as Sidra glanced over at them for a brief moment, he assumed those looks of disgusts were because of what he admitted to the audience. Thoughts of betrayal flooded the general.

"Wisdom demanded it. I mean no affront when I say that anyone who was not there could comprehend the dreadfulness of the battle. I imagine that even our ancestors looked away in horror. I trust that none of you misjudge us," Sidra said and then forcibly shut his mouth. He didn't like discussing battles and war or even war tactics with people who weren't warriors. He believed there should be a sacredness to what he and his soldiers did. Tamrin was an exception only because he hoped to one day include him among the warriors.

But the fact that he sometimes had to explain why a soldier lived or died, or why a certain military decision failed or succeeded to someone who had never fought in battle—and would then turn from the general to discuss something frivolous in their next breath—was truly offensive to Sidra. Now, he was being forced to do so in front of the worst offender in the city.

"How did someone like you come to be a general? How did a man with as much timidity as you become our general? Oh, a fearful general! Tell me, you rabbit! Did any of your men ever yell out for a retreat?"

"No, they did not."

"Did not their muteness tell you anything, Rabbit?"

He didn't reply, but Azmera continued, "It tells me that you should not have ordered that retreat. It tells me that I should have appointed your weakest soldier a general instead of you. The other generals possessed valor and died fighting and never voiced a retreat. I hope you did not stumble over their dead bodies as you fled. Their last prayers were undoubtedly to be avenged, and you denied them that!"

"What I did, I did for the good of the men—"

"And the death of us! Reflect on the message you sent to our enemies! What will they think of our land now? Their foul mouths will say we are fleeing cowards! Their walls will show us as trembling gazelles! Well, we are not. Only you are. Therefore, you returned at night! You did not want the city to see your face in the light. I have never known a general to return from battle at night!"

The crowd became livid. They were talking to each other, something that they rarely dared during an assembly. Azmera was relieved to hear the crowd direct their discontent toward Sidra. It made her feel that they supported her. A flash thought came to Sidra. He wondered where

Khama's support was; he couldn't even find him in the crowd. The queen slowly raised her hand to the crowd to get them to be silent. They quickly became mute.

"Did not wisdom demand you pray to your ancestors?!" Azmera yelled as she looked up at the sky. "Father of Sidra! Father of Sidra's father, why did you not aid him?" She looked back at the stripped general, his face showing his disgust at her insults. "Stories about your actions have burned my ears. You and I will examine each rumor so that I can arrive at the truth." She turned from him. "Now, where is Tizzra?"

Sidra raised an open hand towards the young man, who was standing a few feet away from the other soldiers. Tizzra was the tallest of all the living soldiers, and many women, young and old, thought he was handsome. Azmera let a smile appear on her face as she walked up to him.

"You were the one who saved the lives of the others?" she said as she lightly touched his arm.

After the retreat was ordered, Tizzra directed the men to run into the Nile River, which wasn't far from where they were fighting. They stayed in the river until night. Some of the Egyptian soldiers lingered to see if any of the men would come out of the river. None did. They swam down the river until one of the soldiers was killed by a crocodile, then they left the water, re-assembled, and made their way back home.

"I told the others to follow me to the river after the retreat. It grew dark, and they were riding on chariots, so most did not chase after us," Tizzra told her.

"You, along with the soldiers that died, showed our enemy that we do indeed have strong, savvy fighters among us. Possibly they will realize that their victory did not come from their own strength but our general's weakness. A reward will not be withheld from such a noble soldier! How should I reward you? Land? Jewels?"

"In your palace, you possess a shimmering black jewel. Your servant, Chara. Like every man who has seen her, I would like to have her as a wife," Tizzra said quickly, bringing light smiles and suppressed giggles from the crowd.

The queen hesitated.

"You covet my finest servant? I would give you ten servants! You have my blessing, and *that* is the most valuable thing in our land! But I must require that you make the other soldiers match your strength. You must build them up. Instruct them. Maybe you can be their general someday. Understand?"

"Yes, Azmera," Tizzra said as he fought back a smile. This small dialogue would serve as Tizzra's wedding ceremony.

Azmera secretly wished that Tizzra hadn't asked her for Chara. She wanted the city to start rumors about herself and Tizzra. She wanted to be seen with him in the city and at gatherings. Despite their age difference, she desperately wanted to marry Tizzra, not only to boost the morale of the city, which loved Tizzra more than her, but also to appease the soldiers. She felt that if they saw Tizzra as king, they would believe he would take over the military aspects of governance, even though this is something that Azmera would never allow. Yes, with all the despair and division in the hearts of the populace, seeing Azmera with Tizzra would be a small sign of hope.

However, she could not refuse his request in front of the crowd. After the way she tore into Sidra, she suspected the city didn't want to see her show anymore prejudice to the warriors, especially the best one.

Azmera turned back to Sidra.

"You hold a look of surprise, Sidra. I do not understand why. My advisor's cunning words have convinced me not to have you killed, so instead, I am making you the new prison overseer. Menel, the former overseer, was killed by a prisoner. You may not realize why you lost the battle, but you will understand this: I will never put another decent man's life in your hands ever again. Do you understand?"

Sidra turned away from Azmera. Now, he couldn't even bring himself to look at his wife in the crowd. Azmera looked away from him and addressed the crowd.

"Despite losing the battle, we will still rejoice over our soldiers' return! We will light a bonfire tonight! Everyone in the land will come! Make the preparations!"

Azmera walked back to her palace. Chara started walking toward Tizzra, but she was stopped by the other servants and led back to the palace. The queen's advisor, now visible, stayed in the courtyard. He motioned for Sidra to come to him, but Sidra simply stared at him for a moment and then turned away.

CHAPTER FOUR

At the edge of a nearby village, there was a beautiful lake, called Idrisa, famous far and wide. Foreigners referred to the area not as Queen Azmera's land, but as "Idrisa country" because the Egyptian pharaoh, Idris, visited it many years ago and expressed a desire for it and the surrounding land to belong to Egypt. He died not long after his visit, so his desire was never fulfilled or even considered further. At times, the top layer of water gave a perfect reflection of the blue sky as if it were a wet wavy mirror. The lake was a quarter of a mile wide and about one mile long. Giraffes, zebras, and gazelles frequented the lake because there were no crocodiles in the water.

Sidra, too, was an admirer of the lake. As soon as he saw the leaves of the bordering trees, the scene would smack his senses and demand that he take delight in the view. He liked to come at night, with a torch, and imagine building his palace next to this body of water. After leaving the assembly, he walked to the lake and quickly stripped himself of his feathers, arm rings, headdress, and clothes. He then paused, took several deep contemplative breaths, and with his eyes closed, started to walk into the lake.

As Sidra went into the cool water to end his life, he reflected on his wife. She also loved the lake. He thought about the possibility that his wife would visit the lake after his death. He imagined her sitting on the edge where he laid his clothes and thinking of him. He hoped the beautiful atmosphere, the lake, the swaying, breezy trees, would ease the pain of loss when she visited it.

Khama had followed Sidra. It took but a moment for him to realize what Sidra was trying to do to himself, so he quickly ran into the lake after him. By the time the water was up to Sidra's shoulders, Khama was directly behind him. He didn't waste any words on Sidra; there would be time for that when they got out of the water. Besides, Khama didn't have any words powerful enough to stop Sidra. He simply grabbed the former general and pulled him out of the water. Sidra started to pull away violently until he noticed who was preventing his suicide. Khama kept a firm grip on Sidra's arms and dragged him out of the water.

This was the second time that Sidra faced death in a body of water. In the battle, Tizzra had to push the general into the river, as he was trying to get to his two murdered sons. An Egyptian general found Sidra's sentimentality amusing, so he ran his chariot over Sidra's oldest son, wanting to see his reaction. Sidra broke free from Tizzra, but Heda and two others grabbed and dragged him back to the river. Seeing an Egyptian arrow pierce one of his men snapped the general out of his daze and back to his duty. He yelled for his men to get under the water.

When the two reached dry land, Khama let go of Sidra, causing him to fall to the ground. Khama rested his hands on his knees and tried to catch his breath. He stared at Sidra, who seemed unaffected by the entire ordeal; he was breathing normally as he turned to lie on his back.

"Being a prison guard will not be that dreadful, Sidra!" Khama shouted the moment he caught his breath.

"She spoke truth. The battle may not have been in my hand, but the lives of my soldiers were!"

"Never say so! I never thought so, and neither does the land. She has spoken no truth! Ignore the rumblings at the assembly. The land is not with her. She is the one who has weakened us, not you. Our knees rest in dirt because of her. And yet, I have spent some time thinking about this, and I believe that there is a way that you can toughen the kingdom."

"How?" Sidra asked.

Khama gave a big sigh. He was confident that Sidra would support what he was about to suggest, but it still made him uneasy to say it out loud. Still, his meetings with the returning soldiers and a few guards in the city, had given him a good feeling of how the men felt about the former general and Azmera.

"For many years I have been an advisor. I have done this duty out of love, a deep love for this land. I have given advice so that kings, queens, and generals may help this land flourish and grow. This is the same goal of any sensible ruler; they would all want a strong city to rule over. But now, there is an oddity in our rulership. Something that I do not believe has ever happened before in any land that I know of. A queen who hates her own land. Not one who has simply made mistakes, nor one who would crave an alliance with another kingdom. Our queen hates this land. The warriors, the men. She does not want to see us get stronger; she wants us to fade away. And what are we to do with such a ruler? Reason with her? It has never worked before. Our road is not muddy. It is clear what must be done. I fantasize... a new ruler. For years this land, this air, this sky has cried out for a true leader."

The men sat in silence for a moment. Sidra's breathing soon became heavy. He was excited to hear another's voice saying what was in his head.

"We share a fantasy. In your visions, who do you imagine?"

"Who has been in the palace for many years who will know the course that a ruler must take? I have met with every king or consort that Azmera has seen and some that she has not. I have many alliances through-out the various trade routes who would desire to see me making the rules instead of Azmera. In other words, it would have to be me—but with you by my side as a most powerful general."

"Our dreams are as wasted as the lives of those soldiers who perished in Egypt. I just got demoted to the prison. Prominence is possessed by only one person... Azmera. Death is coming to us anyway. It circles over us like vultures. Who dreams of ruling over a graveyard?"

"It was I who suggested you be assigned to the prison. I did that because I know a way to erase Azmera from the city without us suffering consequences. And the prison is an important setting."

"My ears are yours."

Khama got on his knees and dug his right hand down into the mud by the lake. He scooped up a handful of it and showed it to Sidra.

"Our soldiers have proven that they are as easy to mold as a handful of clay. Their greatest strength is in following orders. This will serve *our* purpose. The clever must lead the strong, lest their talents go wasted. We will mold the land's strongest soldier into a man who will do what we tell him, no matter what it is. This will have to be Tizzra. Before the assembly, Azmera was very inquisitive about Tizzra's welfare. I believe she had her own plans for the young soldier."

"His blade would never graze her skin. Certainly not now since he is probably going to be a general. She dangles affluence in front of his eyes. Still... I do not think he cares for Azmera. He must see her true nature with his own eyes. He must know how badly she has treated Chara."

"No. As we speak, I think he loves her. She must seem like a goddess who is fulfilling his every desire. She has gifted him with praise, prominence, and a wife. We must vanquish his love by making him conclude that the queen is a thorn against him and his new wife. Then he will hate Azmera. He will want to attack Azmera."

"And if he still does not?"

"Then we will have to discuss who the second-best soldier in the land is. But I am sure that it will work."

"He was blessed with a wife today. I do not have to remind you what happens to anyone who leads an attack on our kings and queens. You would put him in that position?"

"After that odious weed is plucked, we would be in charge, and I would reject even the mention of punishment. Give that little of your thoughts, for I have ideas that assure he will not be seized. If evil should conquer, if he did get captured, we could help him escape from the city."

"You want him to kill her?"

"I thought about sending her to Egypt. We will let them know that the only person who longed to attack them is now in their hands. That will reveal to them that the rest of us did not condone the attack. This has been done before in other lands. Our combined wisdom could break Azmera easily. Sidra, she thought nothing about our soldiers' lives. That is why she was able to send them to an absurd battle. If we do not have our revenge, then that would mean that we thought little of them too. Sometimes if revenge is not employed, acceptance and pacification take over the land and grow. It will grow in the hearts of the boys whose father's died in Egypt. And then they will not only have lost a father to show them how to grow, but in his place there will be acceptance, the worst quality a growing boy can have. But we can show them… we can show all these young boys that we do not accept this, and neither should they. Her brow felt no sweat, and her eyes gave no tears when I told her about our soldiers. If not for her dark skin, I would believe that she was an Egyptian conqueror," Khama said as he sat in front of Sidra and put his hand firmly on his shoulder. Sidra thought that Khama was trying to be forceful when he did this and shrugged off the hand. He would make up his own mind.

Sidra liked what he heard about the plan except for the idea of keeping Azmera alive. He thought that her corpse being sent to Egypt would work just as well. And in the instances that Khama was referring to where this had worked as a peace offering, the circumstances were very different. It didn't happen with Egyptians, and the cities making the offering were ten times bigger than the "Idrisa country." Also, according to one of the stories, both warring lands had grown tired of the constant battles and had even entered into a stretch of peace that lasted for years. It was only interrupted by a new young prince eager to make his name known among his contemporaries. The story had been told so many times by so many different people that Sidra was sure that the facts were buried beneath hyperbole. A living queen could cause so much damage that Khama apparently hadn't considered. Sidra reasoned that if she reached Egypt alive, she could tell any story that she wanted, even that she didn't order the attack on them. This would be believable to them since they had good relations with her dead husband, Nospri. *Keeping her alive must ease Khama's conscience about the plan. Though his words are strong, his actions are still of a weakling,* Sidra thought. Nevertheless, he agreed with him up to this point, and he knew that now was the time to act on the idea.

"The plan could live!" Khama shouted in Sidra's ear. "Are we united on this?"

"How long do you think this will take?"

"We must work fast. People will get suspicious if he is gone for too long. We certainly do not want Azmera to know he is contained. We should apprehend him tonight. We must take Chara also. She could tell someone of our movements."

"How long has this idea been in you?" Sidra asked as he looked past Khama and glared at the lake.

"As you and the others marched out of the city, this purpose marched in me. I must admit that I felt as much sadness as your wives did watching you warriors leave because I knew very few of you would return. And you, least of all. But, come listen now. You must hear the rest of my plan," Khama said.

Sidra turned from the lake and looked for the jewelry and clothes that he took off earlier. He put them on with purpose since he now had a reason to live: Revenge. Some men wake in the morning with love in their hearts; others with desires for power or prominence. Sidra's heart, thanks to Khama, was now filled with revenge, a desire that can be stronger than love. Khama and Sidra would do almost anything for revenge—a lot more than they would do for love.

* * *

What gave the city so much hope when they saw Tizzra? Some of it grew from his father's reputation. But a lot came from the fact that most in the land saw something in Tizzra that they admired or wanted for themselves. The young women, of course, wanted to be his wife. The old women and men wanted their daughters to be with him. The older men also wanted his strength applied to their farms to add to their wealth.

Tizzra's wisdom was really exercised when it came to his contemporaries. He would get uneasy sometimes when he would receive praise or gifts while the other soldiers would rarely receive anything.

Tizzra did his best to alleviate the disrespect that this was to the others. If he received gifts, he would give them to the others. He would remind others who praised him that he relied on his fellow warriors to be successful. "Take away their cause for jealousy," his mother would tell him. Now, Azmera had done that. None were jealous of his new position.

Tizzra's strength and reputation were about to be put to the test, not only by Sidra, Khama, and Azmera, but also by the city. True, his strength had allowed him to save many of his fellow survivors, but the city wanted more of him. "Make him a general! Make him a king! Could Azmera marry him? He cannot just be a soldier anymore, he has proven himself, just like Sidra did years ago!"

Azmera too, was very cognizant of Tizzra's appeal and potential. She had no hesitation in applauding him over the other soldiers whether they were present or not. "Give the strong a pedestal to stand on so that others may look upon them with desire. Let them desire to have a man's position, his wives, his strength and favor. This is a healthy thing, a positive side of envy," Azmera had said to Khama a year prior. And no one had more men envy him than Tizzra. Even Sidra had to sometimes calm his jealousy of Tizzra with reminders of how he had made the young soldier successful.

Chara watched all this praise and jealousy. Now his wife, she couldn't stand off from afar and watch what others said or felt about Tizzra; she was going to be experiencing it too. She was now one of the reasons that people would envy Tizzra. Just like his strength or personality, she was another positive thing that people would say about him. It made her proud; like everyone, she had long admired the young soldier. And now, she realized, she had a role to play in making sure that Tizzra stayed envied. She, like Tizzra's strength, personality, and wisdom, was and must remain a positive aspect of his life. His strength must not fail him in battle, and Chara must always be a reason for men to envy him. She must always be a prize.

CHAPTER FIVE

After the crowd had disappeared from the palace courtyard, Tizzra remained outside, waiting for Chara to come out to him. One of the *mundutu* left their tree stumps behind, which Tizzra sat on. The queen had given the new couple several gifts: pottery that Nospri had received from Egypt, which she was happy to get rid of, some clothing that didn't fit her anymore, food, and wine. A guard had brought them outside to Tizzra after they were wrapped in a brown wool sack. While he was waiting, Kito walked up to him waving his hands in an exaggerated manner.

"Your ancestors are indeed the strongest in the sky! They seem to never forsake you!"

"It would appear," Tizzra said as he sifted through the bag of gifts.

"How should I salute our new general? Would you prefer that I took a knee to the ground, or shall I simply bow?" Kito joked with his friend as he bowed his head in front of him. When he raised his head, he noticed that Tizzra wasn't amused. "Why are you not smiling? You will be tomorrow's general! Certainly, you desire this!"

"No. Your 'next' general would make the same decisions as your *old* general. Look upon his fate! Who would seek his tragedy? This is what he fought so hard to get back to: A life of disgrace."

Kito was surprised to hear Tizzra talk like this. Of all the people in the village, Kito believed that Tizzra was the one with the least cause to disagree with anything that Azmera decided on, even if it was to defend Sidra. However, Kito said nothing.

"Do not repeat this, but I think that peace left this land on the day we marched for Egypt. We are going to be saturated in trouble with the Egyptians and our fellow lands because of this battle. We live under gray skies. I have a wife now, and I yearn to be with her, not fighting needlessly in some distant land."

Kito sat down on the ground and thought about what Tizzra had told him. It had been a while since he had even cared about what was happening in the city. Tizzra and the warriors were gone for two days before he even heard about the battle. Kito felt disappointed in himself for this; he should have known about it. After this, he made it a point to keep up better with what was happening in the city. Especially now, since so many were concerned about retaliation from Egypt.

* * *

Inside Azmera's palace, Chara was gathering her things and conversing with the other servants. They were having fun with her, joking about what she was expected to do for her new husband. Chara tried to ignore them; Tizzra was her main focus. Servants such as Chara rarely married. Instead, they were passed around from kingdom to kingdom until they reached an age that made them less desirable as personal servants, and they were demoted to maids or nannies. As she bent over to pick up some of her clothes, Azmera walked into the room and looked at the other servants. They understood the look and left the room. Chara turned around and gazed at Azmera.

"You may have this arm ring as a gift as well," Azmera said as she held out a gold arm ring. Chara kept her eyes on the shimmering ring as she walked toward Azmera to take it.

"Oh. I am thankful to you, Queen Azmera."

"The greatest soldier in the land had a chance to receive anything he craved, and he chose you. How well do you know Tizzra?"

"Our time has been brief, but I do love him."

Azmera looked at her for a moment and then sat down on a nearby stone bench.

"You will carry a heavy heart in a few days. In our land, men care little about how a woman feels. You can love him or hate him. It will not matter to him either way. There will be no regard for your heart," Azmera told Chara.

"I know that many men are like that, but not Tizzra. I am in his heart," Chara retorted.

"He put those words in your ears?"

Chara had to admit to herself that Tizzra had never told her that. However, she didn't want to admit it to Azmera.

"Oh, sheltered girl! Can your fantasies even shadow the highest love there is? Do you know it?" Azmera continued. "Unrequited love. Love born from admiration. When you feel love for someone that you have never seen, or met, or talked to. Do you know why? No stronger love exists. You care for someone even though they have done nothing for you. You love them for who they are, not who they desire to be. And foremost, they cannot hurt your heart. If only my love for Nospri had remained unrequited."

This was the longest conversation that Chara had ever had with Azmera despite her being one of her closest servants. She didn't know what to say and stayed silent. Azmera broke the silence. "Before your spirits are settled, I have a command for you. Offer your ears to conversations about Sidra and me. I need to know how many people truly support him. I cannot trust the murmurs from the crowd earlier. Return here in a few days with some insight. Do you understand?"

"Yes, Queen Azmera."

Chara gathered all her things and walked out of the palace. She saw Tizzra sitting down as he talked to Kito. When the two men looked up and saw Chara, Kito walked off so that the couple could be alone. Tizzra's eyes never left Chara. Azmera was right about many of the other men in the city, but she was very wrong about Tizzra. He did love Chara, but he would never tell her that. Nubian men rarely said such things to their wives. "People are expecting us to be at the bonfire tonight," Tizzra said as Chara smiled at him.

"I know," she replied. The two of them started walking home.

"I plan for my mother to live with us. At least until the other soldiers and I build our home. I did not expect things to happen so suddenly. Understood?"

"Yes, of course. I look forward to her wise counsel."

Tizzra began to ponder his future as he walked. A big part of his future was now smiling and walking with him, but he wondered how he would protect her. A storm was coming, and he was now the one that everyone in the city would look to for protection. He considered his friend Kito. He had successfully removed himself from the city's many tragedies; perhaps Tizzra could follow his example, leave the city, raise a family, and farm in peace away from everyone else. A dream he would consider further. But for now, he would stick around for his fellow warriors, his friends, and the city.

* * *

Kito didn't care too much about the queen's order that everyone attend the bonfire. He wasn't going. He knew as much the moment her words hit his ears. He would not have even attended the meeting earlier if curiosity about the general and concern about his friend Tizzra hadn't gotten the better of him. Kito wanted nothing to do with the city or even the surrounding villages. His home and farm were southwest of the city and didn't sit on very fertile ground, so he did not have any of the arguments with neighbors about territory that many in the village did. No one wanted his land. Kito liked the challenge. The time spent bickering with neighbors was time that should be spent in the field, he thought. This made him feel like he had an advantage over most.

Kito walked home and concentrated his thoughts on his farm. His sons had better be nearly done with the assignment he gave them earlier in the day—to clear the field of any weeds and pests. Kito didn't care about making his sons work in the burning heat, nor did he heed their cries to go with him to the palace to see the soldiers. He tried to show his sons that there was never a reason to be idle. Always be willing to work harder than others. Even when he didn't follow this logic himself, he made sure his sons did.

Kito's boys didn't disappoint him. As he walked up to his home, he could see them hard at work and still angry that they didn't get to go to the palace. It was only by chance that the news about the gathering even reached Kito, he lived so far from the village and city. But one of the city guards was chasing after a returning soldier, pleading with him to stay and meet with the queen instead of fleeing. The soldier agreed to return and stand by his fellow soldiers. Kito heard the conversation and decided to go hear the fate of his friend Tizzra.

It had been many years since Kito attended a bonfire, despite the fact that he loved them very much. Kito was a skilled drummer before his hand was injured, and even now, he loved to play with his sons, though playing for too long was painful. On mornings when he woke up before sunrise, he would take his small set of drums and beat them as he watched the world wake up. Doing so seemed to help him get through his harsh morning routine. The positive effect would wear off as the day went on, naturally. Friends would frequently encourage him to bring his talents to the bonfires, but Kito repeatedly refused, giving an excuse of work that had to be done. In truth, he was embarrassed because of his deformed hand.

He didn't want to get tired playing while the other drummers showed better stamina.

When Kito was young, only twelve years old, Sidra gave him and some other young boys training to be warriors. Like the trial that a man undertook to become a general, the boys were sent out together for days with only spears to defend themselves against predatory animals. There were four boys in this group, and Kito was the oldest. Wise enough not to attack anything too big when they hunted, Kito directed the boys to chase after rabbits or vultures. However, the hunters became hunted when one of the boys chased after a rabbit that a hyena had its sights on. Craving a bigger meal, the hyena bit into the boy's leg, dragging hi with its warm slobbering jaws. Kito and the two other boys did not hesitate to run to their friend's aid, stabbing the animal as frantically as they could with their spears. Three other hyenas stayed in the background watching the episode. Fortunately for the boys, they did not come to their brother's aid, but instead chased after the rabbit that had foolishly considered itself safe. In the melee, the hyena bit Kito's right hand ferociously, shredding the tendons and muscle in his palm. Kito's loud scream made the others focus on the hyena's face. They repeatedly jabbed their spears in the eyes and head of the creature. It stopped moving. Accepted defeat. It didn't fight back in those last moments, just looked up at his killers and died.

The boys picked up their friend, careful not to disturb his leg any more than they had to because of the painful cries he let out. Still, their care was not enough. The severity of the bite and uncleanliness of the hyena's germy mouth was too much for the little boy. His mother held him as tight as she could for as long as she could. Sidra, Khama and the priests looked on as he died. The boy's father did not want to be in the company of Sidra. If Sidra were not a general, the father would have killed him, which he said to nearly everyone who came to comfort him. Kito was also unfortunate in his wounds, though not to the same degree. His hand also was infected, but some of his fingers were amputated, and the infection didn't spread. Since his hand was so painful, he didn't attend his friend's burial. The queen was furious when she heard the story. She ordered that this sort of training of young boys be stopped immediately. People in the city and village applauded this decision. In truth, Azmera was angry about how poorly the boys performed. She also thought the group was too small, reasoning that it should have been seven boys, not four. Still, she limited this sort of test only to those who wished to be a soldier or general.

Despite the praise Kito received for his bravery, he was through with the idea of becoming a warrior. The memory of the young boy dying never left him. That taste of "battle" was all that Kito needed. One of the other boys, Tizzra, felt the opposite.

Kito wanted to keep his boys away from warfare as well. Watching them work on their farm or play outside their hut would cause him to occasionally reflect on the young boy who died. The thought of him lingered like an unwanted guest. But there was no way he would let Azmera take his sons away. This was another reason why Kito chose to live outside the villages and city. His hut was strategically located so that he would see anyone coming towards them from over a mile in all directions.

As his children raced to him, Kito pondered their future. If Egypt retaliated, was he far enough from the city to either escape their wrath or flee to another land? He knew, just like Tamrin, that strange days were coming, but he did not have Tamrin's optimism.

CHAPTER SIX

It was customary for the monarch to meet immediately with the general and the surviving soldiers before the meeting with the entire city, but Azmera wanted to spend some time in her garden first. She went out to it as soon as a servant woke her up.

Azmera's garden was a quarter-mile west of the city. She would occasionally take a female servant with her when she'd make the pilgrimage. Twenty years prior, she had a revelation when she attended her father's burial. Her father, mother, two brothers, one sister, and numerous uncles were buried within a hundred feet of each other. Azmera wanted the strength and wisdom of her ancestors to help her so she planted trees and a garden on the burial site, hopeful that the fruit that grew would contain the spirit of her family.

In times of trouble or when she needed clarity or courage, she would make her way to her garden and conscientiously eat from its bounty. Whether it was a placebo effect or not, her ritual did work. Her mind and body relaxed after she 'consumed her ancestors.' This was more spiritual to her than just staring up at the sky the way the rest of the people in the land did.

* * *

Nearly everyone came to the bonfire that night. Even people from foreign villages came to visit the "mournful city that had lost so much." This would happen every time a bonfire was lit because it would burn so bright and high that it could be seen for miles. Young children danced around the fire, most of them ignorant of the loss that the land had suffered. Sometimes a bonfire celebration would last all night and into the morning, but now the villagers were too beaten down emotionally. The effect of the flames on their neighbors' faces did nothing but underline the somberness of the day. There were also dozens of drummers and dozens of dancers, many of whom were women, due to the lack of men. Nospri didn't have a set size for the bonfire(s), but Azmera gave instructions that twice as much wood would be burned and over a vaster area. In the beginning of her reign, Azmera only wanted the wood from acacia trees to be burned, but she relented on this as the trees became scarce. Now, those in charge of the fire would first lay down leaves and brush and then cover them with the wood. They would begin to collect wood as soon as a bonfire was over to prepare for the next one.

It seemed to Tizzra that as soon as Chara sat down to be with him, somebody would come up to them and steal her away. Lastly, it was one of the older servants whom she had seen only hours before. The old lady wanted to give Chara another present, a piece of pottery that Azmera had given to the old servant years ago. Chara accepted it and made her way back to Tizzra, who was preparing their meat.

Enroute, she passed by an older woman who was sitting next to a recently widowed mother of three. She had her arms wrapped tightly around the young mother as she listened to her weep over her lost husband.

"But I begged! I prayed and begged to every ancestor I had for him. I started praying the day he left, and so did the children, and we did not stop until this morning. I still pray. I plead that my ancestors will bring him back. I spoke to one of the warriors and he could not say for certain that my husband is dead; he may only be missing! They have said that some warriors were separated from the rest on the return home," the woman said loudly, hoping that her words would convince herself. The older woman knew that the young woman was only trying to fool herself, so she held her tighter and began crying too. Her husband was a guard in the prison, so he was still alive.

This scene was taking place all around the bonfire. Older women consoling younger ones. Many of those who were visiting from nearby villages outside of the land could not believe the stories that they were hearing about the fruitless battle. They, too, tried to console the widowed women and fatherless children. Azmera noticed the mood and she would not permit it. She looked at the drummers and raised her arms repeatedly as if to tell them to play louder.

Opposite where Azmera was sitting was a small group of warriors huddling together, discussing the queen's earlier insults.

"In spite of every despicable thing she has done and said, I still cannot believe she treated the general that way… and in front of the widows!" the youngest warrior said.

"That is due to your youth. If you had more age, you would be aware of the horrible things that she said to all of the generals before, including your father. I have seen her slap her advisor for not giving her an update as quickly as she would have liked. If you live long enough you will see her do far worse than she did this morning," a second warrior said.

"It would be more accurate to say, 'If she lives long enough.' Khama's plan, which is much overdue in my opinion, will surely change everything," a third warrior said as he looked around to verify that it was only fellow soldiers around them. "Her wicked words mean nothing now. Let her rail on just as the scoundrels do when they are thrown in prison. Her fate is sealed. Our futures are open."

"But Tizzra— "

"Tizzra shall be given the rewards that he deserves. He would receive them no matter who was in charge. I would not worry about him. He will have the brightest future of all. But first, he must be tested to prove that he is truly worthy of such a blessing," the second warrior declared.

"He has proven himself already."

"He has proven that he is capable of survival. Now he must show that he is capable of bringing the city together so that we all may thrive!" the third warrior said.

"I am one of the few men left in my village. Already, the widows are chasing after me, some for comfort, others for support. Heda's wives have offered me all his belongings and his farm. I do not know how to respond," the youngest warrior said.

"Do not give a reply yet. Offer comfort but no commitment. It would be wise to wait until we know what Khama intends to do with all of the farms of the dead. It may be that their farms will not be as appealing as they seem now," the third warrior said.

A group of young children walked up close to the men, closing down their conversation. They dispersed into the crowd.

* * *

The previous festival had taken place weeks before the men went to war. They knew they were going into a battle, but only the generals and Khama knew it was against Egypt. Some men didn't think it was even going to be a *real* battle since everyone was forced to participate, including the general's sons. The last battle was just a show of power, a pretense, which happened occasionally between neighboring kingdoms. Because of this, the mood was very bright.

The older children would play a game: seeing who could stand closest to the fire for the longest time. Mothers hated seeing their sons play this game, but they rarely spoke up against it because the men encouraged it. At a previous bonfire, a young girl decided to join the boys in the game.

She ran and stood closest to the fire. The men didn't think the child would last long so no one took her seriously until she endured longer than all the young males. Then the men decided to step in and remove the girl, but Azmera forbade it. The young girl's record was never broken.

* * *

Sidra and three guards were standing together. He had assembled them to tell them about an obligation that he expected them to fulfill.

"After the bonfire is over, we have a detainment to make tonight," Sidra explained.

"Who?" one of the guards asked.

"I will tell you later. Keep your lips pasted, for Azmera wants this to be done slyly. Assemble outside the prison after everyone has left from the bonfire."

Sidra walked away. He scuttled by Tizzra, who was sitting with Chara eating the meat from an antelope. He looked at them as he walked past, not saying anything. Tizzra and Chara didn't even notice him. Chara was rubbing the scars on Tizzra's back and legs. Tizzra assured her that they didn't hurt nearly as bad as they looked.

"They are not real wounds from the battle. The general did this. He made us put wounds on each other. Tell no one," Tizzra whispered to his wife and gave her a smile. She smiled back but didn't fully understand what Tizzra was telling her.

The happiest person at the celebration was Tizzra's mother. People tried to be congenial to her and put their own sadness to the side.

The former general was on his way to his wife when one of the queen's guards ran up to him.

"Sidra! Sidra, Azmera wants to see you immediately," the guard said as he gasped for air.

He turned and walked toward Azmera. He had to walk by a con-gregation of recent widows to get to the queen. As he did, many of them stopped mourning and gave him a stare. *Soon*, he thought, *they will stare at me with pride once again.* Azmera was sitting with her advisor and servants, pretending to enjoy the festivities. They were sitting behind everyone else, a position that Azmera had never taken before. She reasoned it would be good to keep her eyes on as many people as possible. When people appeared to be whispering, she noticed. When they did not speak, she noticed. She tried to observe everyone who didn't seem to be enjoying themselves. She was sensitive to the many gaps of silence in the crowd when the drums and singing paused. As Sidra walked up to Azmera her servants and advisor walked a small distance away so that the queen could talk to him alone. Her guards, however, stayed close to her.

"Sidra, I need to tell you that I regret something that I said to you."

"You can hold regrets?" Sidra asked.

"I questioned how you became a general. I should not have said that. My husband appointed you, and my husband always made wise decisions."

"We all make mistakes. You know that."

Sidra couldn't control his sarcasm. It blurted out of him before he had the chance to think about what he was saying. Of course, Azmera was not amused. Even so, she ignored Sidra's implication.

"I am grateful that you did not bring any bodies back with you. It is a rude custom that I would see done away with. A dead soldier has no right to return to his home. I do not know if you have heard about it, but while you were all in Egypt, I sent a messenger to Meroe to ask their king for the loan of some of his soldiers. I presumed that you would suffer losses in the battle, and I wanted us to be prepared. He agreed to send soldiers. I am going to use them as my personal guards. I thought you should know this in case you saw them marching into the city. I would not want you to get scared... again."

Sidra turned and walked off. Normally, the queen would have rebuked him severely for turning his back on her, but even she knew that she had been treating him very badly. Also, she had no wish to cause a scene.

After hours of avoiding her, Sidra finally walked up to his wife. She was sitting with the same women who had been comforting her earlier in the day. When Sidra sat down next to Oja, the other women left. "Is your heart recovering?" Sidra asked his wife. She didn't respond. "Sorrowful words can put a dark cloud in your head and make rain in your eyes. I have a promise to fill you with brightness."

Oja looked at him.

"Our sons' blood will be avenged," Sidra whispered.

She looked away.

Sidra's sons didn't want to follow their father's example and pursue a warrior lifestyle. The oldest wanted to farm; he dreamed of owning the most land and cattle. The youngest had ambition to be a priest. "The priest can control the kings," he would tell his father.

"You are going to kill our sons' murderers in Egypt?" Oja asked.

"Why travel to Egypt? Our sons' murderer is here among us. Celebrating the death of my soldiers! Blaming good men for her bad decisions! Does this make you feel better? When I heard that others blamed her for what happened, I felt better. Many of us have rallied against her injustice. I am doing this to lessen your agony."

"Revenge? Do you remember what my mother used to say about revenge? Revenge is the reaction of a crushed man. No brave man would ever need it." Oja stood up. "And I do not desire to see that boy in our home again! How can you stomach to look at him after our loss?"

Sidra had no problem looking at Tamrin the same way that he did before. He was losing so much that he wanted to hold on to everything that he could, even his surrogate son. Who else could he share his knowledge of war with? Only Tamrin would still listen with interest; Tizzra had heard all his stories and strategies many times before. And Sidra knew it was revenge he was seeking, but he would rather have others call it justice. He didn't bother answering Oja's question about revenge, assuming it was rhetorical. Instead, he got up and looked around the bonfire to see the density of the crowd. Oja's friends returned after Sidra walked off to see Tizzra's mother.

As the queen's eyes scanned over her subjects, she noticed that very few people were dancing or celebrating, so she ordered her servants and guards to start dancing in front of her. Slowly, they complied, but this only satisfied the queen for the briefest of moments. She started pointing to people who she discerned to be wallowing in despair and shouted, "You! Dance!" Her finger landed on Oja, and she hesitated for a moment. Still, not wanting to appear compassionate , she again yelled to the grief-stricken woman, "You! Dance!" One of Oja's friends was next to her and she stood up in Oja's place and slowly danced. Azmera didn't inflame the issue. Khama, disgusted by Azmera's actions, leaned into her ear.

"These souls are beaten. Surely, the celebrating should be done by the Egyptians, not us. Give the people a few breaths to grieve for all we have lost. You must let the land wail. Dismiss the people," Khama pleaded.

Azmera looked him in the eyes. "You! Dance!" she yelled at him.

Khama slowly walked in front of her. He danced. He told himself that this was just an early celebration that he was dancing at. He was about to become ruler of the land. He raised his knees high when he realized that this monster whom he took orders from was about to be overthrown. He stomped with pride as he thought of all the men who were behind him on this. Those men felt pride in Khama as well because they didn't let him dance alone for long. Soon, almost every soldier who made it back from the battle was around Khama, dancing with him to show their support. Khama thought this might be too much support for him and that Azmera would grow suspicious. Yet, Azmera, in her arrogant ignorance, failed to see what was taking place.

CHAPTER SEVEN

There was very little in Tizzra for people to dislike. Just a light arrogance regarding his abilities as a soldier. He would always volunteer for assignments, which the other soldiers rarely did, and then he would attempt (and succeed) to perform them better than others. This he learned from his parents. With Sidra's oversight and encouragement, success was normal.

This put some of the other soldiers in a paradox. The few who didn't like Tizzra were fine with him being brought down a peg or two by Khama's plan. Most others thought about the blessings Khama and Sidra said he would receive when he would be let out.

Each soldier had their justification for Tizzra's imprisonment, and few were conflicted. They were ready for another fight, this one in their home territory, thanks to Khama. A desire for revenge? They had it. A desire to win after suffering a devastating loss? They had it. A desire to change their homeland for the better? They had it. Khama put no encouraging words in their ears before they left for their battle, but he emboldened them on their return. He took a handful of them and walked around the city, showing each the new land they would possess once he was in charge. Eventually, all the farmers, especially those recently widowed, would lose a substantial part of their land to these surviving soldiers. "But not until the conflicts have died down and order is restored in the city," Khama told them.

But what to do about Azmera's new guards? Khama couldn't just have them killed; that could provoke a war with Meroe. And he didn't know what the consequences would be from letting them return safely to Meroe just to tell their king that they failed in their duty to keep Azmera safe. The only logical solution, Khama reasoned, was to keep them in the land for some time until he and Sidra were stronger. Until then, they would be treated as princes, with such honor and luxury that perhaps they would help Khama come up with a story to tell the Meroian king. But that was a problem for the future.

* * *

The prison was a mile away from the palace. It was not visible from the city, and most of it was underground. The entire prison was almost three hundred feet long and fifty feet wide. Each cell was ten feet wide and ten feet long and had very poor ventilation, only a couple of small holes that no grown man could fit his arm through. The floor was not paved; it was only dirt. The cells were separated by mud brick walls. The hallways were lit by torches whenever needed. The top of the prison was covered with crimson dirt and surrounded by a wall of colored rocks. Most of the time, the prison cells were not full. Recently, Azmera had allowed some of the prisoners the chance of freedom if they would fight in the battle against the Egyptians. Only a few volunteered for it because they were aware of how powerful the enemy was. By the time Sidra was given his position, there were only thirteen prisoners left. The entrances of their cells were blocked with heavy rocks.

The prison was a new concept in the land, a by-product of the relationship the Nubians and the Egyptians had. Prior to Egyptian influence, the Nubian version of law and order was swift and moderate. If one stole, one had to pay back double. If one killed another's cow or yak, one would replace the animal threefold. If one murdered a man, one was killed in return. The idea of isolating someone in a small cell seemed useless to society and even the victims a hundred years prior. King Nospri didn't believe in a prison system. He thought it was the shame of civilization. That is why he wanted it as far from the city as possible.

After the bonfire was over, Sidra went to the prison. He walked down the path to the prison's hallway. When he got to the bottom, he saw Khama and three guards waiting for him.

"Sidra. I have words for you before you go," Khama said. Sidra nodded, and the two men walked away from the guards. "This is how you will do it. Azmera gave Chara an arm ring this morning. When you go to seize Tizzra, you will take Chara too. Tell them that Azmera said that Chara *stole* the arm ring from her and demanded that both be arrested immediately. Then put them in separate cells, far from each other. After that, we will turn our attention to Tizzra," Khama explained.

"I understand," Sidra said as he turned to the guards. "We leave."

The three guards followed Sidra out of the prison. The night was warm and still. The moon shone brightly, and the smell of the ceremony remained in the air: the burnt wood from the smoldering fire, the sweet recognizable smell of dozens of antelope flesh (most of it uneaten). Sidra was cautious about anyone seeing them walking up to Tizzra's hut. He continually looked around to make sure that no one saw them. They only carried one small torch with them to not bring attention to themselves. However, many in the village wanted nothing more than to stay in their homes and rest after their long sorrowful day.

Sidra invited Tizzra' mother to his and Oja's hut for the night. He told her that Oja needed to be comforted by another woman, and he didn't want her to be alone while he was at the prison. Tizzra's mother agreed to it since she and Oja had been good friends in the past. Oja was very comforting to Tizzra's mother after her husband died. Sidra's real reason was that he didn't want her to witness them taking her son to prison. Still, he didn't know what to tell her the next day after she realized her son was gone. This was a big problem for him. How could he fix it? *Perhaps Khama will have an idea.*

When Sidra and the guards were in front of Tizzra's hut, Sidra paused for a moment to let all his doubts surface. He mused that the plan was too easy. They must have forgotten something if it only took an afternoon to come up with the idea. However, he allowed his desire to conquer his doubts, then he talked to his guards.

"Display a strong face to him. I have seen him fight four Egyptians at once. He is incredibly strong. And keep your mouths shut. Only I should be doing any talking." Sidra took a deep breath as he turned back to the hut. "Tizzra! Tizzra, come out!" he yelled and then looked around to see if anyone else heard his voice.

Tizzra walked out after a long moment of silence. He looked at Sidra and his guards without saying a word. He was angry at being disturbed so late. Sidra also didn't say anything for a moment. Tizzra thought that Sidra was there to give him a gift of some kind (Sidra gave himself the same rationale: what he was doing *was* a gift to Tizzra). "I will come straight to our purpose. Azmera demands you and your wife be imprisoned," Sidra said, looking down at the ground. Naturally, because of the events that took place in the morning, Tizzra couldn't believe this. He thought he was the best soldier in the land, even better than Sidra. The entire city loved him. And most importantly, he had not done anything wrong.

"She wants us imprisoned? Why?!"

Tizzra was raising his voice, which made Sidra nervous. If he had yelled louder and woke up the villagers below, Sidra would have fled and never returned to bother Tizzra. "Calm your voice, Tizzra. Azmera says that your wife stole something from her. Some sort of ring."

"She is not a thief!"

"I believe you. And in the morning, you and Chara can explain everything to her. But for now, both of you will have to come to the prison with me. I have my orders… as distasteful as they are."

Chara had been listening to the conversation. She took off the arm ring and brought it outside to Sidra. Sidra took it, looked it over, and then handed it back to her.

"It is very nice. You should give it back to her. That would end this situation. You can give it to her in the morning, but as I told Tizzra, I have to take both of you to the prison tonight," Sidra told her.

"But tonight is our first night together!" Tizzra said.

The prison guards surrounded Tizzra and Chara. Earlier, Sidra told them to do this if Tizzra seemed to be resisting. This move did not scare Tizzra; he was willing to fight them all. But Sidra was ready for this. He and Chara looked at each other because they were both on Tizzra's side, and they knew they should work together to calm him so that the guards would not fight him. Chara put her hands on Tizzra's shoulders and whispered in his ear, "We do not want our time together to be ended before it has even begun. Let us go with them. It is only one night. It is just a misunderstanding. This happens with Azmera more than most know."

Tizzra couldn't help calming down when he heard the soft voice he had fantasized about while walking to and from Egypt. The look on Sidra's face also calmed him. Tizzra could see that Sidra was disgusted at himself for what he was forced to do. It was for these two people that Tizzra decided not to fight the guards. He unclenched his fists and tried to calm his mind.

The guards with Sidra stood in silence. They had little idea of what was going on. Khama told them earlier that he would explain things to them later, which sufficed at the time. But now, to be arresting the most loved man in the city, confused them. Khama was leery about some of the guards knowing about the plot. They had stayed behind and didn't see the battle like Sidra did. And they didn't know about Azmera's cruelty as

Khama did, so they would have to demonstrate that they could be trusted. Fortunately, for Sidra, he chose guards who would side with him later.

"You will come with us?" Sidra asked Tizzra.

Tizzra didn't answer. Chara lightly massaged his hand. "We will go with you," she said as she looked at Tizzra and started to lead him down the hill.

Sidra gave a deep sigh as the couple walked past him. He looked around again to see if they were being watched, but there was only the dark night air and silence in the village. He nodded to the guards to escort the couple to the prison. When they left, Sidra walked into Tizzra's hut to make sure that no one else was in there. He noticed that it was indeed vacant, and then he sat down on the floor, which was covered with straw. He didn't want to risk being seen with the guards as they took Tizzra to the prison. So, he decided to wait until they got to the bottom of the hill, then he would catch up with them. As he sat, he noticed Tizzra's father's clothes and jewelry were next to his mother's bed. He got up to touch them but restrained himself and only stared at the items. "Help me, old friend... help me magnify your son," he said.

When they reached the bottom of the hill, Tizzra turned and looked at Chara.

"Did you perhaps take the wrong arm ring by mistake?" he asked her.

"No. She handed it to me, and I put it on in front of her," Chara responded.

"How do you think she made this mistake?"

"I do not know."

At the entrance to the prison, there were ten torches blazing in the night. Two guards were stationed in front. They were instructed to stand throughout the night, but they would frequently sit down on the ground and tell each other stories about other kingdoms, Nubian women, or robberies that took place on trade routes. The two men who were guarding the prison entrance the night Tizzra and Chara were arrested were doing those very things until they saw Sidra and the guards. When they noticed people being brought in, they stood up. Sidra told one of the guards walking with him to run ahead, put out most of the torches, and tell the two guards to walk to the back of the prison. He didn't want anyone to see Tizzra and Chara if it could be prevented.

As Tizzra and Chara walked through the prison entrance, Sidra walked up to Tizzra to lead him to a cell at the end of the hallway. Tizzra assumed that he and Chara would be together in the prison, but instead, she was led to a different cell, four away from Tizzra's. By the time Tizzra noticed that Chara wasn't going to be with him, a guard was already placing huge stones in front of the entrance to his cell.

As Chara was taken to her cell, one of the guards who wasn't with Sidra when he performed the arrest, a man named Bon, recognized her. He used to work in Azmera's palace.

"Chara? Chara, why are you here?" Bon asked.

"Because of a misunder—" Chara said before she was interrupted by Sidra.

"Go away! Her business here is not your worry, guard!" Sidra yelled.

Bon stared at Sidra for a moment and then walked away. He looked back at Chara as he walked up the path to go out of the poorly ventilated prison. Years earlier, he was an overseer in the palace until he had an altercation with one of the king's former advisors. As punishment, he was made a guard in the prison.

"It is bettter that most people do not know that you are here. You do not want rumors to spread, do you?" Sidra said as he slowly looked at Chara. "You may not know it, but she has made mistakes like this before."

"I know she has. But those mistakes were understandable. This is senseless!"

Sidra looked at her and said nothing. He tried to look sympathetic to her, but it didn't work. Chara caught herself and remembered that she was still talking to one of Azmera's subjects.

"I am sorry," she said. "My lips have betrayed our queen."

"You are only speaking the truth. The truth should never be hidden or considered betrayal."

Sidra suddenly realized that it would be advantageous to have Chara hating Azmera also. Perhaps her words would encourage Tizzra more than his or Khama's could. "Did you know that there are tales about you and the other servants in the palace? I have heard that when foreign guests visit the palace, you and the other servants.. were instructed… Well, anyway, she let certain rumors spread among her advisor and generals. But worry not; I am sure that Tizzra has not heard about it...yet. I would like to keep it that way, and I am sure that you would too. He does not require disappointment in his heart."

Chara said nothing. She walked up to one of the cells.

"Is this mine?" she asked.

Sidra nodded, and Chara went inside. He had had her cell prepared for her. He tried to make it as nice as possible for her—a small blanket and a large crack in the wall that would give her the occasional cool breeze. Tizzra, however, had the worst cell, for Sidra wanted him as uncomfortable as possible. When he walked out of the prison, he saw Bon sitting by one of the now relit torches. "No one is to find out that they are here. If you reveal anything, you and your family will be put to death... Do you understand?"

"I do," Bon replied, confused and hesitantly.

Sidra turned and went back into the prison. He walked to Tizzra's cell, removed the rocks blocking it, and walked inside. "I will be seeing Azmera in the morning before I come back here to get you. I did not want to convey this earlier, but you might be here longer than one night. I cannot express how infuriated she is over this missing arm ring. I am not definite if I can persuade her to see you, but I will do my utmost."

"How could she make this error? She has known Chara more profoundly than I have. She knows that she would never pilfer anything from her! Chara still has the ring that she gave her. She will give it back," Tizzra said. Minutes earlier, he had mulled over the possibility that Azmera had him arrested because of his lackluster response to being a general.

Sidra stepped out of Tizzra's cell for a quick moment to see if anyone was listening. He stepped back in when he saw no one.

"It is time you realize who Azmera is and what she is trying to do. She craves notoriety. She lusts for statues of herself, just like the kings in Egypt. While you are in here, I want you to ponder her actions and decisions. She will forfeit all of us just so she can become renowned. That was what the battle was about." Tizzra looked down at the ground. It didn't matter to him if what Sidra was saying was true. He just wanted peace for himself and Chara.

"The number of people who have had enough of her tactics is swelling. There is talk that some people are trying to remove her. Possibly even kill…"

"That is another man's saga! It has nothing to do with me! Sidra, please get me out of here."

"I will."

Sidra walked out. Down the hallway, he saw Bon standing next to Chara's cell. He walked up to him and told him to put extra rocks in front of Tizzra's cell and reminded him not to have any contact with Chara. The former general didn't worry that Bon would talk to someone about what he saw because the threat of a man's family being killed was usually enough to keep him in line.

* * *

Sidra's love of the Idrisa lake took hold of him before he was a general. When he and Tizzra's father, Pnogi, were both soldiers and best friends, they would practice tactical maneuvers by the shore. These were peaceful years, and the royals didn't pay much attention to the army. Their members were small, equipment shoddy, and training pathetic. Most of the generals were more concerned with their farms than army warfare.

Still, Pnogi was gifted. His spear would almost effortlessly make its target. He had more speed and agility than anyone else in the land. In his hands, a spear could pierce the eye of a charging lioness. Skill-wise, Sidra was always two steps behind Pnogi, but there was no jealousy on his part.

King Nospri's last trip to Egypt should have been an uneventful one. He had made it many times before and with a limited caravan. But now, because of Azmera's urgings, he would take more men with him for safety. Unenthused by the age and physique of the generals, he appointed Pnogi and Sidra to be his chaperones. The other generals protested this so much that, in anger, Nospri pointed to Sidra and yelled, "You see?! This man is now a general! I give him the title and privilege to accompany me in my travels! If there is more any of you want to say about it, I will make him head over all of you!" The other generals became quiet. Sidra didn't have to prove himself to the others through tests from the other generals. He didn't have to receive a blessing from the priests either. No, his blessing was given in answer and received unceremoniously. A 'congratulations' look from Pnogi was all the celebration that Sidra would get.

Pnogi was glad that he was not appointed in this way. He wanted the trials, the priests' blessing, the bonfire ceremony to announce him. He presumed Sidra wanted this for himself too, but he was wrong. Sidra didn't care how he got it as long as he got it. The two of them prepared well for their trials to prove they were fit to lead.

Pnogi had a goal to finish the trials in ten days, setting a record. The quickest anyone completed the trials was twelve days. But Pnogi was stronger than any of them, and he was able to complete the task.

The king's caravan arrived at Mox, a small village several miles away from Egypt, Nospri ordered the caravan to stop. Turning to Pnogi, he said, "You go ahead and announce to the city that King Nospri is arriving tomorrow. Announce that we are on a goodwill mission and bring gifts for the pharaoh." The king waved his hand at his caravan, indicating that they were to camp where they stood. Pnogi had no clue how to do what Nospri asked or where to go. Nevertheless, he took off running toward the city. As the caravan settled, one of Nospri's soldiers who had been in the village for a day approached the king. While some kings and pharaohs preferred giving their host more time, Nospri felt that a day's notice was all that was required. He would make judgments based on how well he was received; if he was offered much on his visit, he would applaud the city for its generosity and abundance. Conversely, if given little, he would size up the city or village as detestable (maybe conquerable) and would rarely travel or receive travelers from there again.

The soldier told him that he made arrangements for the king. He had spoken to the elders; they knew Nospri well due to his travels to Egypt and other cities that brought him through their village, and they prepared a modest feast for him as well as the most comfortable bed they had.

As the king laid down for the night in a bed, the rest of the caravan stayed by the camels and donkeys and horses. Burdened on these animals and a few men were the gifts that were to be a given to the pharaoh. Nospri was worried about being forgotten or overlooked by Egypt because of their distance and location. He didn't want his people to be behind in trade, innovation, education, or warfare. "Since the rest of the world goes to Egypt, we must go to Egypt," Nospri reasoned. And his gifts were extreme. Dozens of garments for men and women, hundreds of pounds of different beans, a large assortment of crystals, exotic fruits and seeds which no longer exists. General Sidra stayed awake most of the night to watch over the caravan. Still excited and wanting to prove himself, he made sure that no one took anything they were not supposed to. He also kept an eye on the livestock and animals that were in tow, walking in between them.

Meanwhile, Pnogi had made it into the city near dawn. He was indecisive about who he should approach with his message: a soldier, a citizen, a priest, someone black like him. Who to choose? He settled on a soldier, and this was the correct guess. The soldier brought him to his general, who in turn took Pnogi to a priest. Only after receiving the priest's blessing and being disarmed of his spears and blades was Pnogi allowed to see the pharaoh's house servant. Pnogi gave him his message, and the servant passed it on to the pharaoh. Accommodations were made for Pnogi; he slept in the house of the soldier who he met first.

Pnogi lay in the soldier's bed, displacing the soldier to another room. He wanted to sleep so he could be ready to receive King Nospri the next day and show that he fulfilled his assignment completely. Pnogi was impressed by how well he was being treated and reasoned that if they received a messenger this well, they would welcome a king one hundred-fold. But three things kept Pnogi awake, and he could see them well from his bed. The Pyramids. There were small pyramids or ziggurats in Nubia, but they paled in contrast to Egypt's. The design and greatness stirred Pnogi's soul.

Azmera had seen the pyramids years prior to Pnogi. Her prejudice prevented her from feeling anything complimentary about them. "We have many pyramids, not just a few. I prefer Nubia's. It is easy to stand on the backs of slaves and proclaim greatness for oneself." These comments and many more were made not only to Nospri, but to any Egyptian she spent more than an hour with. She repeatedly ignored Nospri's demand that she desist in her insult. So, for the final two days of their visit, Nospri restricted her to the pharaoh's palace.

The next afternoon, the caravan arrived at the Egyptian palace. The pharaoh and Nospri both praised Pnogi for handling his assignment so well. Afterward, Nospri had his gifts presented, doing so in a manner that made the pharaoh uneasy. He would have preferred to examine the gifts privately rather than in front of Nospri. Still, he was happy with the gifts and the king's visit. It was on the return voyage that events became dire.

Pleased with how Pnogi handled himself as a messenger, Nospri decided to use him again to inform the same village elders in Mox that Nospri would be returning the next day. Forgetting that he appointed Sidra a general, he commanded him to accompany Pnogi. As the two friends waited in the village for two days for the king to show, they began to grow impatient. So did the village elders. This was not the normal actions of the king. If he knew he would be delayed, he would have sent another messenger to let the elders know. Pnogi and Sidra knew that something must be horribly wrong. One of them must travel back to determine the delay. Sidra suggested Pnogi do it because he was quicker. Pnogi didn't debate the issue; he ran off immediately, leaving Sidra to deal with the angry elders who were starting to question if he and Pnogi were who they said they were.

"We know many of the generals, and we have never seen you before," one of the elders said.

"I was recently appointed."

"I did not see you when the king left us days ago."

"I stayed with the caravan, watching over the animals."

"How many days did it take you to finish your trial? What sort of gift did you bring the queen at the end?"

Sidra knew this last question was a trick. The queen wasn't given a gift and not even allowed at the ceremony; neither were any other women. Sidra wanted to lie to the men but decided against it in case Nospri would be angry at him for doing so when he arrived. So, he told the embarrassing truth.

"I was not appointed through the trials, but by King Nospri himself. And the queen receives no gift at the end."

The elders turned to each other to discuss Sidra's answer. Unsure as to whether or not a king would announce appointments this way, they decided to trust Sidra for a little while longer. But he would not receive the same courteous treatment that the previous messenger did. He was given table scraps for food and slept on the dirt floor outside of one of the elders' hut.

Thoughts quicker than Pnogi's feet ran through Sidra's head. What should he do if the elders decided to attack him while he slept? If he fought back too adeptly, he could cause strained relations with the village and King Nospri. This would look bad as his first assignment as a general. And where was Nospri? Or Pnogi? Pnogi knew the situation was tense when he left; he should have been back. Sidra tried to calm his nerves and get some sleep, but the clanking of metal coming from the elders' hut piqued his curiosity. Slowly and stealthily, he pried his fingers through the straw to look into the hut. He saw two of the elders whispering quietly, their spears tightly clutched in their hands. It was time to run off. Sidra looked around him to determine his best route out of the village, but before he could decide, the elders and younger men spotted him. Any way out would have to do now. Sidra grabbed a nearby torch and began running as fast as he could. As he ran, he set fire to all the huts he passed, hoping it would slow or deter some of the men following him. It worked, but not as well as Sidra hoped. Spears began to whiz past his head, telling him not to run in a straight line. The cries of the young men and the fires woke the entire village. The women started to put out the fires.

Sidra was able to lose the attackers by hiding in one of the huts he had previously set on fire. He waited for the large group to pass his hiding place, then he snuck out. A woman with a large bowl of water saw him.

"He is here! He is here!" she yelled and would have been taken more seriously if other women weren't erroneously yelling the same thing all through the village. Sidra threw his torch at her, causing her to drop her water and run off. Sidra ran in the opposite direction, thinking that it was astonishing that he was still in the center of the village and unharmed.

This is my trial. This is my trial. I will not fail it. Even if I must burn the entire village. A calmness flowed through him as he realized how inept the elders were. He reasoned that if he had another torch, he could burn every hut on his way out of the village.

It was time for him to find Pnogi and the king.

The next afternoon, Sidra ran up to the fractured remains of the king's caravan. Decaying bodies were strewn about, similar to the king's ransacked luggage and gifts from the pharaoh. Sidra quickly reasoned that the king must have been attacked by no less than twenty thieves, possibly following him out of Egypt.

The general ran from dead body to dead body in search of the king and Pnogi. Despite the fact that a few of the men Sidra encountered were still clinging to life, he ignored their pleas and continued his search for his friend and his king. He turned over the body of one of his fellow generals who was still alive.

"Where is the king?" Sidra asked.

The general pointed his hand to a covered body. "There." Then he pointed his hand to a covered dismembered head. "And there."

"Have you seen Pnogi?"

The attempts to talk took too much out of the dying general. Blood pooled in his throat, and he choked on it, still trying to give Sidra information. Unaware of what he should do next, Sidra turned the man on his stomach hoping it would let the blood run out of his mouth easier. But the loss was too much for him to recover from.

Sidra had to confirm the king's death for himself. After cautiously looking around for any more bandits, he walked over to the king's head and took off the silk cover. It was indeed the king. Even though he was not there when it happened, he felt a spirit of disappointment was emanating from the king's head, giving the general a chill through his body, but strangely, not his head. He covered it back up with the silk cloth and walked over to the king's body. It was uncovered, naked and had over a dozen arrows sticking out of it. Sidra surmised that thieves had taken all the camels, donkeys, and horses except for the three that were lying dead on the hot ground. Vultures had already started in on the animals and some of the men. Sidra scared them away when he could, but the feast was too much for them to forfeit. Sidra did protect the king's head and body by putting them in one of the king's broken caravan compartments.

The new general felt the gravity of his situation. It appeared he was the only survivor, and since he could not find Pnogi anywhere, no one could verify the events he saw. The incident in the village did little to help. As the evening relented to the night, Sidra decided he would again check the bodies for anyone alive. He found none. He began to look through the king's personal compartment, which had obviously been ransacked. He remembered that when the pharaoh gave Nospri his gifts, Nospri placed one of them in a hidden drawer in the bottom of his compartment. It was covered by common wool, which is why the thieves didn't bother taking it like they did all the other upholstery, made of deerskin.

When the drawer wouldn't open, Sidra went out to find a large rock to hit the drawer with. As he retrieved the stone, he looked again at the dead comrades on the ground. He noticed the farthest body from him had no vultures on it and wondered how this could be. Still, he gave no great consideration to it and went inside and began beating the drawer loudly until it opened. Inside was a small fortune. Rubies, gold statues, and small silver bars were piled inside. Sidra's awe gave way to the realization that the reason the 'dead soldier' didn't have vultures near him was that he wasn't dead or a fellow soldier. The same moment Sidra realized he was a thief, the man burst into the compartment. Sidra quickly grabbed his spear and thrust it at the thief but missed. The thief responded by throwing sand in Sidra's face and then grabbed the drawer and ran off. Sidra knew this gift from the pharaoh gave credence to his story that he would have to tell the queen. It would demonstrate that he had no part in what happened and did not gain from the king's death. He needed those jewels to succeed. He wiped his burning and itching eyes, grabbed his spear, jumped out of the compartment, and ran after the thief. His lack of sight made him leery of any shape he saw since it could be another thief. Still, he followed the sound of the jewels and gold in the drawer rattling around. His vision began to get better. Just as the sound of the drawer stopped, Sidra thrust his spear at the figure, thirty yards. Direct hit! Right into the center of the body. Sidra heard the drawer drop to the ground. He stopped running and took a moment to wipe his eyes so he could see clearly.

What he saw then made him lose faith in his vision. On the ground was the thief with a spear stuck in his chest—Pnogi's spear, he now realized—and next to him, still standing, was Pnogi, Sidra's spear in his back. Pnogi stood above the thief, holding the drawer he had just picked up.

The general dropped to his knees in disbelief. Pnogi was still standing. Sidra came to his senses, got up and ran to Pnogi.

"Pnogi! No! No!"

"Was there another bandit? Be aware!" Pnogi struggled to say before falling to his knees.

Sidra wanted to lie. To tell him someone else struck him, but he couldn't. The wound from his spear was an accident— the wound of a lie would be deliberate.

"I could not see. He threw sand in my eyes. I thought you were him!" Pnogi looked at Sidra and then down at the tip of the spear poking out of his chest.

"No. There was another bandit. You must tell everyone so when they ask. Hurry home. There are more thieves coming. I escaped them. Go."

Pnogi could say no more; his punctured lung was filling with blood. He pushed a mournful Sidra away and lay down on his side. Sidra knew his friend well. He knew he wouldn't let himself die without seeing Sidra walking away. So Sidra gave him his dignity. He grabbed the drawer, stood up, and ran off for five minutes. When he knew Pnogi must be dead, he came back and buried him. Sidra left his spear in Pnogi's back; he would never touch it again, but he did take Pnogi's spear out of the thief's chest. He also took one of Nospri's rubies and placed it in Pnogi's hand.

"For the wages," Sidra said, referring to an Egyptian death belief.

The next afternoon, as Sidra was returning, he saw on the horizon over a hundred generals and warriors marching in his direction. Queen Azmera had sent them. Three of the king's caravan escaped the attack and made their way back home. They didn't stop at the village for Sidra because they didn't want to be delayed. The queen at once dispatched the best men in their army to hunt down these thieves and ascertain the fate of her husband.

The thieves were never found.

The general was pleased to see the army and yet apprehensive about telling the other generals and the queen the news. However, his fears were not justified. The generals already assumed the king was dead and Azmera tearfully went into her chambers when Khama told her about Nospri.

The other generals later lauded Sidra for his savvy in dealing with the elders in the village and the robbers he encountered. The generals sang his praises through the land, resulting in others chiming in too.

Thus began Sidra's lust for admiration. He soaked up every positive word he heard about himself and reflected over every compliment. It became the heart of all his actions. He needed it to do his duty to the best of his capabilities.

* * *

Sidra left the prison and went back to the lake where he earlier tried to kill himself. Khama and Tamrin were there waiting for him. Tamrin wasn't married, so he didn't have to worry about finding an excuse to tell a wife. Khama didn't bother telling his wife anything; he simply walked out. Dawn was hours away when Sidra met the two at the lake. He was very tired since he hadn't slept much in two days.

"What did he say? Will he undertake it?" Khama asked Sidra before he had the chance to catch his breath.

"He is not ripe yet. I think that he will do it because he certainly has fire in his eyes, but I question if we are prodding him in the right way. He will strike out like a cornered lion. We want to make sure that when he does strike, it is at the right person."

"Time slips from us. At the bonfire, I learned that Azmera expects to see Chara in a few days. You will have to increase his suffering," Khama uttered.

"Perhaps we should think about using someone else," Tamrin said.

"No. This entire land loves Tizzra. Pride is attached to his name! People need to see that he is with us," Khama told Tamrin as he walked up to Sidra. "His pain must be increased. Do you not agree, Sidra?"

Before he could answer, Tamrin interrupted, "I have a thought! I know something we could use!"

The two men looked at each other. People had doubted Tamrin's intelligence for many years. Now, he finally had the chance to prove himself. He wanted the same acceptance from the village that Tizzra had received so easily. If Sidra had only believed in him, he would have gone after Azmera himself.

CHAPTER EIGHT

Tamrin was an oddity to the two young boys when Sidra first brought him home. He was dirty, scared, and there was still blood on him, some of which got smeared onto Oja's otherwise clean floor. Oja gave the little boy a long stare, decided he was a cute child but had no other opinion of him.

"I thought the queen would have wanted him, but she declined. He will stay with us now," Sidra said, resting his hands on the little boy's head while he stood behind him.

"Why must he stay here? For how long?"

"It will only be temporary. There are merchants passing through the city in a few days. I will have them take the boy with them as they head to Egypt."

Sidra's oldest son walked up to Tamrin.

"What is your name?"

"Tamrin."

"Have you seen a red grasshopper before?"

Tamrin gave no reply. The youngest chimed in.

"Come outside. We will show you!"

The three boys went out of the hut.

"Make one of the soldiers take care of him. We do not have the room or food for him," Oja said.

"He is staying here. The queen has given provisions for him. His family were merchants traveling to our city. They were ambushed by robbers. It would put a bad taste in all the traveling merchants' mouths if the city neglected the boy. She wants it known that he received the best treatment possible from the best family in her land."

Oja said nothing. She looked around for extra food that she could prepare. Sidra stepped outside the hut and looked at the three boys playing with insects in the dirt. A smile finally surfaced on Tamrin's face, something that hadn't been there since before his family was killed. A smile appeared on Sidra's face also as he watched his two sons play with Tamrin.

Perhaps another boy in the home will toughen up my sons, Sidra thought. He had noticed that his sons didn't play much with other children. Sidra used to think this was because of his status; children were told not to play too rough with his boys so as not to be responsible for any injury. Then, he noticed that no other generals' children were being treated in the same manner. This revelation filled Sidra with more confusion than anger. Tamrin would be good for them. He could show the other children in the land that they could play well with others.

* * *

Sidra, Khama, and Tamrin quickly walked up to Sidra's hut. Tamrin and Khama waited outside as Sidra took a deep breath and went inside his home. He looked at Oja and Tizzra's mother, who were both sleeping on the floor.

Khama leaned into Tamrin and whispered into his ear. Tamrin's eyes widened as he took the object that Khama slyly handed to him.

"Wake up! Get up!" Sidra said to the two women who woke up groggy and dazed. "I yearn to speak to you," Sidra said to Tizzra's mother.

She collected herself and stood up. Sidra put his hand on her shoulder and led her out of the hut since she was still groggy. When she saw Khama, her eyes widened, and her senses grew more alert.

"What have you confessed to her?" Khama said, noticing her look.

"Nothing yet," Sidra replied.

Khama paused for a moment and then walked up to Tizzra's mother. Sidra, again, looked around frantically to see if they were being observed.

"The queen has detained your son. Her guards came after him and his wife. Aside from his freedom, he bellows only for you. Come and see him now."

Tizzra's mother was too shocked to say anything. She finally bowed her head and allowed Khama to take her hand and lead her away from Sidra's hut. The four of them walked out of the village without speaking a word. Sidra, especially, was trying to be very quiet so that they would not wake anyone.

They didn't take her to the prison where Tizzra was lying awake on the ground, thinking about Azmera. Instead, they took her near the lake that they had been visiting so much lately. The sun was starting to rise when the four of them stopped. Tizzra's mother didn't know what to think about what was going on. She, like most of the people in the land, trusted Khama even more than Azmera. Khama knew this and expected it to fuel the rebellion.

"I do not see Tizzra here, Khama. You said Azmera had him," Tizzra's mother said.

"You will see him in a moment," Khama replied. "But first, there is something that we want to discuss with you, and since time is fleeting, we will not be shy about our purpose. The city is dying and so is the tolerance for Azmera's arrogance. There are plans to kill her. There are plans to overthrow her. We cannot safeguard her from these rebels who wish her harm. What we can do is strike her before they do. These rebels' plans are short-sighted, but ours is not. And we desire your son's help. The land loves him. If he is the one who overthrows her, the city will support us."

"Even an old king would not disregard his mother's advice. Let him know that if he helps us, it will bring unimaginable glories to him and his young family. A man like Tizzra deserves no less," Sidra proclaimed.

The weary woman was now in even more shock than before. She was mostly surprised at Khama; she thought that he was Azmera's friend.

"What mother do you know that would encourage her son to kill?" she said.

"You have encouraged him to kill before," Tamrin said in a stern tone. "I saw the two of you before he went to Egypt. You were—"

Sidra put his fingers in front of Tamrin's face. No matter what genius idea he would come up with, Tamrin would not get the respect he deserved from these two men. At times, he felt as unappreciated as Azmera did. Even so, Sidra was right to stop him. They didn't want her to be defensive; they wanted her to be understanding and cooperative.

Tamrin was referring to the day that the generals and soldiers left the city. As wives and some elderly fathers said goodbye to them, Tamrin loitered around the entrance to the city that Sidra would have to pass through. In his heart, he hoped that his adoptive father would secretly tell him to come along with them, to fight beside him and Sidra's sons. As he waited, he looked over at Tizzra and his mother. She was holding a spear that belonged to Tizzra's father, Pnogi. She implored Tizzra to take it with him into battle, but Tizzra refused. He told her that he didn't feel that his father's spear or shield should see battle again without his father holding them. In truth, he felt his spear was superior and didn't want to deal with keeping track of his father's equipment. Tizzra's mother relented but told him to do everything he could to come back to her. "Kill as many as you have to so you may see another day," she told him as she held him in her arms.

"Whatever Tizzra craves, he will get. If he wants to be a general, he will. If he just wants to farm, we will give him as much land as we can. He will not be able to discern his dreams from his reality. And you, too, will get whatever you hunger for. We shall see to that! We only plead that you talk to him and endeavor to persuade him," Sidra said as he put his hand on her shoulder.

"If the city loved any of us like they love Tizzra, then we would do this ourselves and not upset you," Khama said.

"Do not be afraid to be revolutionary!" Tamrin interjected.

"People are expecting me to be behind something like this. That is why I must distance myself from it. If ears hear that *I* was participating, the motive would appear merely revenge. It is a woeful thing to be a contamination! I do not have the land's admiration that your son has," Sidra said.

"Egypt will rule us if we do not pursue to make peace with them very soon! Do you think that Azmera will try to make peace with them? Tell Tizzra to kill her! Shield your village!" Tamrin yelled at her.

Sidra once again put his hand in front of Tamrin's face to silence him.

Khama walked up to her slowly and tried to talk in a sympathetic tone. He wanted her to believe that she could play a large part in this scheme.

"We are desperate. Look at me. You must surely inhale our desperation. I have been the queen's friend for many years, and now here I am emboldened to see her gone. Tizzra does not have to kill her. For now, we just need to have him take her out of the land until Sidra and I establish what should be done with her."

"Will you assist us?" Sidra finally asked.

As was her usual, Tizzra's mother took her time in responding. She repeatedly looked at the men in front of her, one at a time, as the sun's fresh morning rays rose in the background. Finally, she looked down at the ground.

"No. I will not aid you."

Sidra was the only one who felt disappointed. He looked her in the eyes and again started to ramble about all the reasons why she should help them. Khama and Tamrin took a few steps away from Sidra and Tizzra's mother and began whispering to each other. After some brief words with one another, Tamrin pulled a piece of braided rope from around his waist. Tizzra's mother wasn't paying any attention to Sidra who couldn't see what Tamrin and Khama were doing because they were behind him. When she saw Tamrin tightening the ends of the rope in each of his hands, she decided not to fake an interest in Sidra anymore and ran off. Tamrin caught her, dragged her to the ground, and started strangling her with his rope.

Sidra couldn't believe what he was seeing. He pulled out a sharp blade and started running toward Tamrin. Khama quickly grabbed him and told him harshly to let Tamrin finish. Sidra put his hands on his head and fell to his knees as Tizzra's mother stared at him, dropping his blade on the ground. Their look of shock was so similar that, for a moment, Khama thought Sidra was mocking the poor woman.

With morning birds chirping in the trees, a warm sunrise taking place in the east, and morning dew forming on the ground, the breath of an innocent woman had been stopped forever by a boy whom she barely knew.

Tamrin stood up, staring at the body. He felt satisfying seconds of pride in himself for having the courage to do what he did. Later, he reasoned that although he wasn't given a chance to prove his allegiance in battle, he would be allowed to show it in ruthlessness. The young man had no problem with that, as long as his service was appreciated. Not wanting to look at Sidra's disapproving face, he turned towards Khama, who only gave Tamrin a nod of approval. Sidra got hold of himself long enough to speak again.

"What did—why did you do that?!"

"We needed her help. This way will accomplish more than her words could. Tamrin, pick her up," Khama spoke.

Tamrin didn't think that Tizzra seeing his mother strangled was enough. When Sidra went away to find a cover to wrap the dead woman's body in, Tamrin approached Khama. "Tizzra would be very hurt if her body was littered or foul smelling."

"Do what you want with her. But do not touch her face. I want him to have no doubt it is she," Khama said as he walked out of view from Tamrin, who began picking up the dirt and leaves around him.

CHAPTER NINE

The sun had been up for two hours when Sidra made his way back to the prison. The guards outside saw the covered body that Sidra was bringing inside, but none of them would dare lift the cover to see who was underneath. As Sidra walked into the prison, he told every guard he saw to leave. As they walked past him and the body he was carrying, they got a strong scent in their nostrils. When Sidra reached Tizzra's cell, he laid the body down on the ground and started removing the rocks from the entrance. Afterward, he stepped inside the cell. Tizzra was sitting on the floor, eager to get out and confront Azmera.

"I am avid to go. Will she see us?" Tizzra asked as he stood up and wiped the dirt off him.

Sidra didn't speak; he just hung his head. Tizzra let out a huge sigh and sat back down.

"What did she say?"

"When noble spirits abandon a city like they have ours, wickedness has no restraint! Your plight has become worse. Look what Azmera did !" Sidra said and then quickly stepped out of the cell and picked up the covered body that he had been carrying from the lake. He laid it on the ground near Tizzra and then took the cover off. Cold, prickly blood sped through Tizzra when he saw his mother lying dead on the floor. "Look at what Azmera did!" Sidra repeated in a whispering tone to make sure that no wandering guard could hear him.

Once the disbelief was gone, the tears arrived. Tizzra covered his face with his hands so Sidra wouldn't see him. He quickly crawled to his mother and gazed over her body. Through his tears, he started talking to Sidra.

"Who did it?"

"Azmera."

"No. Which of her guards killed her?"

"I do not know. Earlier this morning, she dispatched a messenger to come and get me. When I advanced into her palace, your mother was lying spiritless on the floor as if she were a decoration. Azmera ordered me to show her to you and then bury her."

"Unreasonable! For an arm ring?!" Tizzra yelled as he looked up at Sidra who said nothing in reply. "Discover which one of them did this to her! That is the only man I want to see."

"You know this is about more than arm jewelry. Perhaps you did not show the proper enthusiasm as our new general. Perhaps she wants her new guards from Meroe to take our place. Still, you have more imperative matters to consider. Your wife may be following your mother. Wickedness has ignored her so far, but you now know how unsound Azmera can be." Sidra felt that now was the time to tell Tizzra the entire plan. Tizzra's thoughts of anger and revenge were surfacing, they needed direction. Sidra walked to the doorway and blocked the entrance.

"I am your friend, Tizzra, as I was to your father. I will succor you and your wife as much as I can. But as my hands are weary, I am limited in vigor, so I will not cloak my desire. Recall last night when I told you about all those people who want to see Azmera devoid of power? I think your place is with them. No. I *know* your place is with them. If I could get you out of here, would you...grab her?" Sidra wanted to say, "kill her," but changed his mind at the last second. He assumed it would be too big of an ask, considering how emotionally raw he was from his mother.

"You can get me out of here?"

"Getting out is simple but staying alive would be hard. That is why you would have to get rid of Azmera first, before she could find and kill you. The entire land would be desperate to find you. And I, along with the other guards, would be put to death for failing to keep you imprisoned."

Tizzra raised his hand to Sidra.

"Give me solace," Tizzra said as he looked at his mother.

Sidra reached to pick up the dead body, but Tizzra grabbed his hand.

"Leave her here with me!"

Sidra laid the body back down on the dirt floor and quietly walked out of the prison. When Sidra was outside, one of Azmera's guards ran up to him.

"Sidra! Azmera wants to see you urgently. Some men from Meroe have arrived and Azmera wants you to meet them," the guard said.

"Did she tell them that I was not a general anymore?" Sidra asked.

"No, I do not think so. They seemed excited to see you. Perhaps she did not want to disappoint them," the guard replied.

"Perhaps she did not want them to see how ludicrous her decisions could be," Sidra uttered under his breath. He regretted saying this as soon as the words were out of his mouth. He turned to look at the guard to see what his reaction was. The guard said nothing, as if he hadn't heard, nor did he look back at Sidra.

* * *

As a young, eager man, Sidra tried his best to blend in with the other generals. It took him weeks to find the long ostrich feathers that the rest of the generals wore. He also searched through many carcasses for the teeth (incisors only) that he would make a necklace and arm ring from. His search was too productive. His teeth were longer and bigger than all the other generals, a fact they did not take well. One evening they surrounded him.

"All must give praise to young general Sidra! He wears the most prominent adornments of any man save our departed king!" an old general said.

"Ah yes. Let it be known that even though we fought for our lives and land while he was still nursing, he is now grander than all of us. His necklace shows it," a second general lamented with a loud voice.

Sidra knew this wasn't going to work. Being a new general, he couldn't afford to be isolated from the other generals. He needed their knowledge, guidance, and wisdom. He needed to know the secrets about the land and the military that they possessed. Still, he thought, one day he would stand over all of them. They were "easy to beat," he told himself. So full of jealousy and bitterness. But until his day came, he would have to be subservient.

"You tease me too well. For I do hope to hold your experiences as my own one day. Doing so would give justice to me wearing this necklace. But this necklace is not for me," Sidra said as he took it off and extended his hand. "This is my gift to my fellow generals."

"Which one…" the second general asked as he was interrupted by the first general grabbing the necklace from Sidra's hand and laughing as he put it on. Sidra still had a few loose teeth that Oja was going to make into an arm ring. When he went home, he took one of the teeth as a measuring tool: he would not have any teeth longer than it. For the time being.

Azmera, on the other hand, wanted all the generals' teeth on their arm rings and necklaces to be as long as possible. "Make the enemy wonder," she told Khama. The larger the teeth, the bigger the conquered beast, was her reasoning. Khama agreed, and by the time Tizzra was a soldier, all the warriors wore them. Tizzra and most soldiers hated the teeth arm ring because it would dig into their arm, becoming a nuisance.

In combat or skirmishes, they would try to make sure that their arm ring would break quickly.

One aspect that the soldiers could and did thank Sidra for was the ostrich feathers. Always shimmering black. Always longer than a man's hand. Always to be worn over the groin and wrapped around the knees and worn as a headband. The feathers weren't an interference like the sharp incisors, so the soldiers made sure that their feathers were clean, long, and presentable. Tizzra had an idea to wrap a few feathers under his arm ring so it wouldn't be such a bother, but one of the generals forbade it, believing that the feathers were too precious and rare and beautiful to be covered by anything.

The ostrich had been seen less and less during Azmera's reign. Underfarmed and overtraded, Kham reasoned. Azmera, naturally, blamed the Egyptians for their disappearance.

* * *

Azmera and her new guards were standing in the center of her palace. When they saw Sidra, many of the men beamed with approval. They walked to greet him.

"General Sidra! I am Rethe. We have all gleaned many stories about you. We feel honored to be subject to your command," the young soldier said.

"I savor your admiration, Rethe. But you will not be under my authority. You will report directly to Azmera."

After Sidra said this, he noticed that the faces on the new guards looked puzzled. Before they could ask him questions about why they wouldn't report to him, Sidra quickly changed the subject.

"Did you just arrive?" he asked the soldiers.

"Yes. Not too long ago," Rethe responded.

"You men must be drained and thirsty. Such a long distance you have traveled just to—I will see if I can have something brought to you."

"Go up to the roof to rest, and *I will* have something brought up for you," Azmera interjected.

Not saying another word, the new guards turned away from Azmera and Sidra and walked up the stairs to the roof. "I shall have to teach those men some respect and courtesy," Azmera said.

"I am sure you will be a good teacher of those qualities," Sidra said as he turned to walk out of the palace.

"Sidra! Do not depart without telling those men the truth about yourself! Go upstairs and tell them that you are no longer our general. And tell them why."

Sidra hesitantly started to walk up the stairs as Azmera watched him. A thought of strangling her popped into his mind, but he pacified it with the reminder of what he was planning.

"And, Sidra...I caution you, if you endeavor to make me look foolish in their eyes, you will pay for it... with your eyes."

"I will not *try* to make you look foolish in their eyes," Sidra said as he continued up the stairs.

The morning was very bright, and nearly everyone in the land was already awake and at work. Many people tried to do most of their hardest work in the early morning or late evening so that they wouldn't have to work so hard when the sun was at its strongest. Azmera's foreign guards were sitting on the flat roof looking at the people working in the land.

When Sidra reached the top of the stairs, he stood there for a while and did not say anything. The guards didn't see him because their backs were turned. Sidra took a deep breath and prepared himself to once again address a group of soldiers and watch the respect they had for him disappear from their faces.

"Men... there is something that I neglected to tell you." The men stood up and walked eagerly up to Sidra, making his task even harder.

"I am not a general anymore. Azmera reduced me to a prison overseer yesterday. We just came back from a battle in Egypt, which I am sure you heard about. In said battle, I ordered a retreat, which Azmera did not applaud, so she demoted me."

"If you are not a general, then who is?" one of the guards asked.

"No one. All the other generals died in the battle, alongside my two sons. Azmera is plotting to make one of the soldiers who fought with me in Egypt the next general. His name is Tizzra."

"Can we gather with him?" Rethe asked.

"I will try to arrange that as soon as possible," Sidra said and quickly walked down the stairs.

As Sidra walked down the stairs, disturbed by what he was forced to tell the men about himself, Azmera called for him.

Could they be turned? Sidra considered the possibility since he could feel the respect they had for him before they knew of his disgrace. The footsteps a general, especially an admirable general, leaves behind are the pathway that a soldier plans to walk in. Sidra's footsteps were well known. Perhaps the sands of shame and demotion hadn't covered them completely. Maybe the most courageous stories about him had reached their land and left such an impression on these Meroeian soldiers that they could muster up more respect for Sidra, enough to follow him over Azmera. The look on their faces suggested as much.

Still, they were an unknown. A big risk. If they were to support Sidra and Khama, or even just look the other way, the plan would certainly succeed. Tizzra wouldn't even be needed. But if they clung to their duty and their instructions from their king in Meroe, then the plan would be all that more difficult. No, Sidra knew it was best to leave them out of it. There was no way to determine for sure where their loyalties were, so they must be regarded more enemy than friend.

"What do you want, Azmera?"

"Tizzra. I heard you discussing him upstairs. I sent a guard to his home earlier, but no one was there. Do you know where he is?"

"I have not seen him since yesterday at the bonfire. If I see him, I will tell him that you are looking for him."

Azmera said nothing further to Sidra, turned from him, and walked away. Deep in her heart, Azmera was sure that Tizzra had fled the land. She knew that he had gotten what he wanted and that he would have no peace if he was forced to be a general. Tizzra was wise to ask for Chara in front of a crowd. Azmera soon regretted her quick release of Chara, now that Tizzra was nowhere to be found. The fact that most feared an Egyptian retaliation was no secret to her, but she hoped that Tizzra, her favorite soldier, would not be scared of invasion. The sooner Tizzra was found, the better.

* * *

Back on the roof, the foreign guards became very concerned about the situation that they had been sent into. They did not need to talk because they knew all of them were thinking the same things. Before they left their land, they had heard rumors that Azmera's army was planning to attack a city near Egypt. Then two days later, they were told to relocate to Azmera's land to help maintain order while most of the military were gone.

As the guards looked upon the land from the roof, they realized that they saw very few young men working. Most of the males that they did see working were old men and boys. They also noticed a lot of women comforting one another. Although polygamy was accepted and even encouraged in the land, many men only had one wife since these were not prosperous times.

From the roof, one was able to see for miles to the north. Straining one's eyes would allow one to just barely see the entrance to the legendary caves. The legend of the caves was that once one entered or dwelled in the caves, one could not leave as the same person. Entering the cave was also comparable to asking one's ancestors to abandon one. Interestingly, nearly all of the men who returned from the battle felt that their ancestors did abandon them, but they still wouldn't consider entering the cave.

Patches of over-grown vegetation contrasted with barren fields were noticeable to the guards. They knew those patches told a heart-wrenching story about a dead soldier who would tend to his small piece of land no more. Perhaps this soldier's widow was too overcome with grief to do anything in her husband's field. In any case, the guards saw the physical land was just as beaten down as the people left behind. These were the scraps left by war—too insignificant to the enemy to destroy. This was a feverous infection, caused by battle, now running its course on the land and people.

Rethe stood up and walked away from the other guards. Finally, he expressed what most of the others were thinking. "This is what it looks like after a storm. Such an extinct land! What breed of queen would hurl most of her men to attack a powerful country like Egypt?"

Delo, another guard who was a good friend of Rethe, stood up and walked up to him. "If we tarry here too long, she will casually sacrifice us as well. Anyway, it is only a matter of time before the Egyptians turn up for their revenge. And the foremost person that they will come for is the person that we are supposed to shield with our lives."

"This may be true, but I do see another way out of this. Perhaps things can be swayed so that this land will be taken by Meroe. I do not imagine that Egypt will attack here then. Azmera must grasp this too. Maybe that is the true reason that she sent for us. She is saturated in arrogance, not stupidity."

"I am not convinced. A small city like this attacking Egypt does not sound like a smart strategy," Delo said as he looked over the land.

"True," Rethe said as he also looked over the land. "I wonder what kind of soldier would be hesitant to be a general?"

"One who fears what the future holds for this land. Or it could be he does not have faith in the queen's resolutions. Who can fault him?" Delo replied.

"See, if we stay here too long, we will come under attack from the Egyptians. One of us should go back to Meroe to tell General Sacho what is truly going on in this land. I do not imagine that the queen has told him the truth."

"Let us send Rupdra back home tonight. I will tell Azmera that we are sending him to get more men to guard her. Then, when Rupdra gets back here in a few days, we will know what the king wants us to do."

The two men called for Rupdra.

* * *

It was only for appearances that Rupdra ran out Azmera's city gates. He did so only to impress Rethe and Delo. Two miles out, he stopped running and even took a long break, not thinking that his assignment was an important one, despite Delo's urgings. It could and would have to wait until Rupdra rested and replenished himself. The reason he was sent in the first place was because they could manage without him. He was the dimmest soldier in the Meroeian army. The general who sent him to Azmera was glad to be shut of him for a while, much to the chagrin of Delo, Rethe, and the other guards. Accidents typically happened around him and there was little patience for that. Rupdra himself knew that he was thought very little of. That is why he assumed that Delo and Rethe would not give him anything important to do.

On foot, the journey would take about three days each way, being over a hundred miles away. The terrain was mostly flat except for twelve hills that Rupdra would have to cross.

When he saw familiar ziggurats in the distance, four days after his trek began, Rupdra ran into the city, again for appearance's sake. He zipped by the traveling merchants carrying their assortment of dates and nuts. He sped through the marketplace, hoping that all who knew him would see him and speculate as to why he was back. He ran up to as many guards as he could, asking them where the general was. They all told him the same answer: in the general's home, but Rupdra still ran around frantically, gathering attention along the way. Finally, a palace guard grabbed and shook him and told him to report to the general's home immediately. Rupdra ran even faster.

The general was outside of his home, repairing the straw on his roof.

"General! General, I bring news from the Idrisa land. Rethe has sent me. Please hear me."

The general was displeased to see Rupdra. He thought immediately that Rethe was being humorous by sending him, his least favorite soldier.

"Speak," the general said wryly.

"Queen Azmera. She moves strangely. In a battle, she sent nearly all her generals to their death. The only one to remain has been demoted. There are almost no men in the land. No one wants to lead her army anymore. They are in a peculiar situation. And it was Egypt. The battle was in Egypt!"

The general threw down his straw. "Egypt! She lied! Come. We see the king!" the general said as he pushed Rupdra into running.

The two men ran to the entrance of the palace and disarmed themselves of their blades and spears. A palace guard escorted them into the center of the palace and instructed that they wait for the king. An hour later, the king showed himself. He had the sort of arrogance and haughtiness that Azmera would look up to. He was a good friend of Nospri, and the two would share and swap objects and people all the time. Azmera thought this would continue after Nospri's death, but it slowed down significantly.

"What is he doing here?" the king said, pointing to Rupdra. Even the king had disdain for the young soldier.

"He brings news of Nospri's land. Things are not well."

"That is why they were sent. Because things are not well."

"It was Egypt she attacked. All her generals are dead!"

"Egypt?! Bring our soldiers back! We must sever ties! Go."

The two ran out of the palace. The king rested against a wall as he thought of the possible implications of this news. As he pondered, his small grandchild ran up to him with a large beetle in his tiny hands.

"I caught another! A bigger one!" he said as he showed it to his grandfather.

"That is a big one, Piye. Go look for another one!"

The little boy ran out, leaving his grandfather to his contemplation.

* * *

Later in the afternoon, Sidra was inside of his home eating with Tamrin. The ground was totally covered with straw, as were the walls. Unlike most people in the land, Sidra had a very comfortable bed. The roof was very large, over ten feet high.

The custom in the village was to never eat inside of the home. However, on this afternoon, Sidra and Tamrin were inside eating antelope meat. Oja was not there, but he told Tamrin that he would have to leave before she got back. Sidra was still disgusted at Tamrin for what happened earlier with Tizzra's mother, but he didn't mention it to him yet. He was shocked to see that Tamrin had it in himself to murder. The man thought about how bad he had treated Tamrin in the past and couldn't understand why Tamrin had never tried to kill him.

Without announcing himself from the outside (to avoid suspicion from Sidra's neighbors), Khama walked into Sidra's home. Tamrin jumped when he saw him enter.

"Sidra. What regarding Tizzra? Will he do it?" Khama asked.

"I have made advancement. He does detest her now," Sidra responded.

"How much longer is this going to take?" Khama said, reaching down and grabbing some of the antelope from Tamrin's hand. He started tearing off chunks of the fragrant meat with sharp teeth.

"I wish that I could answer that. I am letting him have the remainder of the day isolated with his mother. He wanted that."

Khama threw down the antelope meat.

"We do not possess time for that!" Khama yelled. "What if he—"

"Consider! He has to sense that I am alongside him and that I will assist him. Besides that, he deserves it." Sidra gave a loud sigh and walked outside of his hut. A moment later, Khama did the same.

"I, even now, cannot believe you did that. It was his mother, Khama," Sidra said as he gave Khama a look full of disgust, something he never dared to do before.

"I did that as a sacrifice for my kingdom. Years from now, even Tizzra will value what I did, I believe. That is, if he were to ever discover it."

Sidra's arms started shaking when he thought about Tizzra's mother. He was reminded of how dangerous and ambitious their plan was. Nubian warriors were prepared to see death, but all the deaths Sidra had seen recently were of people who didn't deserve it. Azmera was willing to kill innocent Egyptians as well as her own soldiers. Khama was willing to kill Tizzra's mother to serve his purposes. And both were willing to use Sidra as their puppet.

"No! He must never uncover us. We must make certain of that before all else," Sidra said, looking around to confirm that no one was listening. Sidra's fears of being overheard were justified. Some years before, when foreign trade was more welcome in the land, Azmera had talked her husband into killing a family that she viewed as disrespectful to her and the land. They would not attend any of the king and queen's bonfires or ceremonies. The father was a very strong and smart man whom Azmera wanted in the army. He refused, preferring to work on his farm (similar to Kito). Azmera had him killed and gave his farm to Khama. The man's wife and children went to live with his brother. It soon became no secret that the man's children, one nine years old and the other one eleven, were planning to avenge their father. Azmera heard about this and had the children killed in front of the city's inhabitants after a bonfire celebration. Later, she warned the people that she had spies spread throughout the city to monitor conversations and everyday activities, staring at her husband while she gave that warning. Ever since then, the people have been afraid to speak badly about Azmera in front of others. In truth, Azmera only had these spies until Nospri's death. After that, they were dismissed, but no one knew except Khama. Even the spies thought that they were being replaced.

"There is an additional factor I wanted to talk to you about," Khama said as he looked back at Sidra's hut. "Can we trust him?"

"Tamrin? He is dumb, but true. He will do anything we say," Sidra said.

"I know he is dumb. We do not need any dumb errors to transpire, so be cautious what you divulge to him. And do not give him too much to shoulder."

"I will be shrewd."

"Tomorrow I will come to visit you. I will require you to have Tizzra's complete support. If not, then we will have to talk about a new plan. One that does not involve Tizzra."

This was Khama's way of saying that they would have to kill Tizzra and Chara if he didn't help them.

"Now, I have to go," Khama continued. "Azmera wants me to meet her new guards."

After saying this, he turned and walked away.

CHAPTER TEN

The young girl, Rado, took a long time to process what had happened to her father. She was joking with him only minutes earlier, but now eight sharp spears were sticking out of him. Six in his backside, two in his front. His shock mirrored his daughter's.

He was a palace guard until two months prior. His failure to continually keep the torches lit roused Azmera's ire. She ordered he be dismissed and thrown in prison. Khama and the other guards thought this was too extreme a punishment. Khama removed him but he didn't throw him in prison. The man knew nothing about the prison decree. One day when giving a speech to the city, Azmera noticed the man in the crowd. She later asked Khama why he was not still in the prison. Khama confessed that he did not completely obey her order.

"You have skimmed the land of my justice. There must be a punishment. Gather all the guards who worked closely with this man," Azmera said.

The queen looked over the eight men who were the former guards' friends. Khama stood in the background.

"I gave Khama an order that your friend be dismissed and thrown in the prison for some time. He disobeyed that order. Now, my anger is unquenchable! All of you will take your spears and pierce your friend, because of Khama's disobedience."

Khama walked up to the queen and fell down on his knees. "Oh, Queen! Forgive me! And please let any punishment come upon me, for my own mistake! For none of the others ever knew about the prison decree!"

"You have demanded this! Your actions have caused this! You wanted to protect him—you have killed him!"

"This man is their friend… since they were children. Please do not put this deed in their hearts."

Azmera lightly touched Khama's face as she bent down to him. "I could have made the same plea to you. All of this is a response to your doing. I thought my judgment for him was merciful. But, no, not even my advisor would allow me to be kind. This is why a queen must show half the mercy and twice the seriousness of a king. Now, arise and carry out my orders."

With that, Azmera walked to her chambers, followed by two of her servants. The guards stared at each other and Khama, still dazed. They were surprised that Khama would take to his knees on behalf of anyone; they had never seen him show such behavior before. Initially, most of the guards admired his actions and appreciated that he would probably do the same for them. However, after the sentence was carried out, they felt that perhaps he didn't do enough pleading.

Anything but pleading would have had a better chance with Azmera. She was also surprised that Khama would think it would sway her. She later decided she was glad the entire incident took place. Khama needed to see the consequences, not only of his questionable loyalty, but his inability to persuade Azmera. "He should have argued better. Longer. Stronger. It was a man's life and he let me take it with only a few whimpers while his friends watched."

Still, as always with her rage, hindsight revealed a plethora of better ways the situation could have been handled. She no longer trusted her palace guards. She overlooked their loyalty to her and focused on their betrayal of their friend. The queen no longer wanted any male guard inside her palace after the incident. They were to remain outside unless told otherwise. She would send communications to them through Khama or a female servant. Of course, she felt differently with the new guards, for they didn't know her.

Minutes after her father's death, Rado stared at the men responsible. She had played with all of their children; they were her friends. She had been in all their homes, and they in hers. As she knelt by her father, she was unaware of the long screaming that she was instinctively providing. At the same moment that she reached out to touch her father, one of the guards picked her up and turned her away from the corpse. Meanwhile, another guard bent over and wiggled all the spears from the body. The other guards watched from a distance. The little girl was released after the other guards started walking away, having each received their spear, and three women had approached the body to begin the ceremonial burial procedure.

Burial customs in the land were unique to the person and how they died. If a death was considered natural, from old age or a stillbirth, it was believed that the ancestors called for the death because they needed the qualities of the individual—the wisdom from an elderly person or the innocence of a baby. They needed these attributes to fight against dark forces on the other side of life. If one died by accident, it was because they were also needed abruptly for a cause.

The former guard still qualified for a guard's burial. Even though Azmera agreed on this point, her non-compliance would not have stopped the other guards from showing a respect for their friend's corpse that they failed to show for his life.

So there, on top of the ground where his body lay, Rado sat every day for two weeks. Her emotional being was rocked; she couldn't believe that someone she loved so much was now gone. And her logical mind couldn't comprehend how it all happened so fast, so effortlessly. A woman said, "Kill him," and moments later, he was dead. But if it could happen to her father, who was the strongest man she knew, then it could happen to Azmera as well. Everything she knew about her father told her that he would want to be avenged.

Over the next month, Rado devised her plan. She knew the only time she could get anywhere near Azmera was at a bonfire or ceremony or meeting. She would not have to wait too long, for the queen called a meeting that all in the city were obliged to attend. Rado knew this to be her one and only opportunity. She had been practicing jabbing and thrusting movements with her father's spear and had gotten very decent.

On the meeting day, Rado had snaked her way through the crowd to the edge facing the queen and her entourage. She had broken her father's spear in half and covered the sharp blade so it wouldn't brush against anyone.

Despite her care, Rado was spotted by the same palace guard who pulled the spears out of her father's body. Grabbing her by her shoulders, and interrupting Azmera's speech, he tossed her to the ground, simultaneously taking her father's spear from her hand.

"What is this?!" Azmera asked, angered at the guard for the disruption. The guard didn't want the girl exposed to Azmera's wrath. He was prepared to give the queen an excuse and then chide Rado later in private, but Rado spoke up.

"This is for my father!" Rado yelled as she jumped on Azmera and bit her neck. As the queen screamed in pain, her guards pulled Rado off and pinned her to the ground.

"You are not even worthy to die from my father's spear!" Rado said as she reached for the spear that had fell to the ground in the melee.

A stunned crowd watched as Azmera stood up and walked to Rado, her hand covering the fresh bite mark. She picked up the girl's father's spear and handed it to the aforementioned guard. "Kill her. Use her father's spear. And all of you must watch! See a traitor's reward!"

The guard hesitated as he looked into Rado's eyes. He'd be responsible for killing a father and his child. More than just a father, his friend. He barely had it in him once and felt he couldn't do it again. Still, he tried. He reminded himself that the girl should be responsible for her actions. She brought her death on herself because she gave way to revenge. Also, she had to know that she wouldn't live through this. 'She must be ready to die since she did all of this so openly.' A memory of Rado laughing and running around his home as she played with his son flashed through his head, but since it was unwanted, he shook it off. He needed a justification that he could tell himself at the moment and in the future. *It would be best if I did it, so none of the other men have to go through what I must. I will absorb the horror. And my hand is the steadiest and strongest of all the guards. I can make it quick for her.*

That was all the guard needed to tell himself. He had his courage. The crowd gasped as he fulfilled his orders. Azmera was sure that some would disapprove of her actions, and she had no patience for their emotions or opinions, so she dismissed them, urging them to disperse quickly. When left alone with her guards, and after ordering that Rado's body be burned (a taboo practice that wasn't even done to conquered enemies), she gave them orders as she held a bloodied cloth to her throbbing neck.

"You will find this rodent's family and have them killed too. I will not suffer murder attempts by everyone she shares blood with. You may do what you want with her family's belongings," the queen said as she turned to walk inside her palace. A concerned Khama escorted her.

It had been decades since a regicide attempt. It was also unsuccessful. Khama spent a lot of his time trying to calm and restrain Azmera. She had pondered killing all the family's closest friends as well, including Rado's young friends. Khama reminded her that Rado's friends were her palace guards' children, and she wouldn't want to kill her guards' children. Doing so, he assured her, would certainly risk further and more dangerous assassination attempts. Reluctantly, she agreed and restrained herself. This was the beginning of Azmera thinking that she should have different guards. Foreign, single and childless would be ideal for her. "I am to be their life. Their desires should be to serve and protect me and only me," she thought.

* * *

For twelve hours, Tizzra sat in the corner of his cell crying as he held his mother's corpse. He tried to ignore the pungent smell of her stiff body. Even though she had been dead for less than a day, her body gave off such a strong odor that it was noticeable to many in the prison, including Chara. The guards were bothered by the smell but were ordered by Sidra not to touch the body until Tizzra requested it. At nighttime, a man in the cell next to him, Embe, had grown tired of the odor.

"You! Are you awake?" Embe yelled to Tizzra through the clay wall that separated them. "Do you know where that odor is coming from?!"

"I have a dead body in here with me!" Tizzra yelled back.

"Yell for a guard so he can take it out of there!"

"No! I do not want them to take it! It is my mother! Azmera had her killed, and Sidra brought her in here for me to see one last time! Our hearts are not ready to part yet."

"How much longer do you plan to gaze at her? It is time that you have her buried!"

"Just until the morning! I want more time with her!"

"No one in here can sleep with that smell!" Embe said, quickly realizing that he was talking to Tizzra in the wrong manner. "What is your name?!"

Tizzra didn't answer.

"My name is Embe! I am sorrowful about your mother, but you had better venerate her! You should recall her as your beautiful mother, not a decaying corpse! You know that the earth now calls for her. Yell for one of the guards so she can be buried!"

Tizzra again did not say anything in return.

"Would you like for me to call the guard for you?!" Embe asked.

Tizzra knew that he couldn't hold his mother forever. The smell had been bothering him as well, but whenever he thought of letting her go, he would remember that this was his last chance to see his mother, ever. Even so, the time came for him to stop focusing on his feelings and to start respecting his mother.

"No, do not call for the guard!" Tizzra yelled to Embe. "I want to bury her myself! In here...with me!" Tizzra carefully laid his mother down on the dirt floor beside him as if she were lightly sleeping. Then he crawled to the middle of his cell and started digging in the ground with his hands.

Down the hall, Chara could hear the cries of her new husband as he wept over his mother. Confused as to what could be causing this, she thought he was being tortured and that she would be next. Teeming with anger, she took a rock and began pounding on the arm ring she blamed for her troubles.

After the ring was flattened, Chara sat back in the corner of her cell. As she breathed heavily, she considered what Azmera's motive might be in having her thrown in prison. She reflected on the passing comments that some of the other servants made about Tizzra. She remembered how they would joke about Azmera wanting to marry Tizzra herself just like most of the women in the land. Chara reasoned that this must be her plan: Have them both arrested, force Tizzra to marry her instead by threatening to keep Chara in the prison—or worse, kill her. *Perhaps she will persuade him by allowing me to be in his concubine. I was stupid to believe that she would allow her best warrior to marry her best servant at a time like this. Giving in to Tizzra's request may have made her look generous to the crowd earlier, but I know her true motive! She wants him for herself! She wants to make him a king, not a servant's husband! This must be the reason for her ridiculous speech about unreturned love. She was trying to prepare me!* The young woman's anger built up in her again. She picked up the dented arm ring and was about to fling it against the wall again when she realized that she should be more practical. It was gold. If she were to get out of the prison, she would need something of value to get out of the city. If she were not to be with Tizzra exclusively, she would not stay at all.

"What did your mother do to Azmera to merit death?!" Embe asked in a bored tone.

"She did nothing! Azmera has lost her senses! She thinks that my wife pilfered from her, so she is aiming to punish my family! She may try to kill my wife and incinerate my home!"

"Where is your home?!" Embe asked.

"On top of the southern hill! It is the only house on that hill! My father built it so we could look down on the entire village! That home is all that I have left to remember my family! She had better leave it alone!"

"I am sure she will! Now, dig!" Embe said as he lay down on the ground to sleep.

Tizzra said nothing. Instead, he continued to dig his unsuitable grave for his mother. Hours passed before this task was completed because he kept pausing to reflect on all that his mother would miss. She had always loved young children, and Tizzra had one day hoped to have many children for her to entertain. But all that was gone, and when Tizzra reflected on that, his emotional pain progressed to a physical pain in his stomach.

CHAPTER ELEVEN

"We must delve deep within ourselves if we are to succeed in this. Our enemies are as sharp as a blade. And if we are to fail... for you, there will only be a stern chiding. But for me, there is only my death," Khama had told Azmera years prior in reference to their plot to get rid of the other two advisors.

The conversation took place over a month before Nospri was killed. Khama and Azmera were of the same mind about many things back then, whereas the other two advisors typically disagreed with them. Adding irritation to this, they were both Nospri's childhood friends and remained close to him for a long time.

Nospri wanted a bigger kingdom, and he thought an alliance with Egypt was the best way to achieve this. His childhood friends agreed with him. Azmera and Khama did not. "He should be looking west, not north," Khama told Azmera. They felt that if any alliance were to be formed, it should be with the black-skinned kingdoms, Meroe and Takhuum. Egypt opened them up to too many unknowns. "And why should we turn away from our gods and start worshipping cats and eagles and other deities that would occasionally end up as our dinner? First, a strong, black-skinned kingdom must be set in place, then we can consider friendship with other kingdoms," Khama told the king as the other two advisors listened.

"And who among our 'black-skinned' friends should we appeal to, Khama? Not a year ago we were challenged by the Uuma tribe. The Asumba have hated us for as long as memory can serve. And Meroe… true, they have been our friends for many years, but they have no desire for more than that. They crave no alliance with us," the first advisor said.

"Yes, Khama. They crave no alliance with us, but they do wish for it with Egypt. Imagine two friends racing to a nugget of gold. No matter who reaches it first, there can no longer be the same trust between the friends as before. For the winner will always be suspicious of his friend trying to hurt him and take the gold, and the other will be suspicious and envious of his friend for what he will do with the gold. We and Meroe are the two friends. Egypt is the gold. Yes, we will stay friends until one of us reaches Egypt first, but then…" said the second advisor.

"Yes. You must listen to them, Khama. They are holding all the wisdom this time. We must put our kingdom in the lead and then we may help Meroe into the alliance. But we must win. We must be strong all our days. We must walk with the strong, learn their ways. We already know the ways of Meroe and the other 'black-skinned' kingdoms," Nospri said to Khama as he looked across the hall to see that Azmera was listening in. He would scold her later for doing so.

"Ah, but remember, the scorpion does not hunt with the snake. The lions do not travel or lodge or kill with the pack of hyenas. And why not? Because there is too much fear and misunderstanding. There could never be trust between a scorpion and snake. But consider, if there were many scorpions, legions of them, that surrounded the snake and then offered to hunt together, the snake would have no choice but to accept the scorpions' invitation. Anything less than legions of scorpions, and the snake may prefer to fight than submit," Khama retorted.

"But we are not scorpions, and they are not snakes! We are men, as they are, with more similarities than differences," the first advisor yelled as he walked up to Khama.

"We are. The four of us in this room are sensible men. And we have met with most of the tribes and nearby kingdoms and know most of them also to be sensible men. But who could say that of the Egyptian pharaoh? Only twice has he seen us, and always with an attitude of curiosity. Never as he would receive an Assyrian king. We must turn that on its head, and only numbers can accomplish that. We must have more with us when we see the Egyptians again," Khama said, knowing in his heart that he was talking to three men who had already made up their minds. He reasoned that now it was time to reach for a smaller victory.

Azmera stood behind a wall, trying to avoid the men's sight. She thought about what she would say if she were Khama. They had spoken about this conversation Khama was having with the king beforehand, but both hoped that he would be alone, no advisors to bring up counterpoints. Not that Nospri needed his advisors; his mind was already made up.

"At the least," Khama continued, "let me travel to the other kingdoms to get a sense of where they stand on an alliance. I would be most discreet and would never mention your hopes regarding Egypt to them. Then, with all the facts in hand, my king, you will have made the wisest decision."

The two advisors quickly glanced at each other. They had the king's ear because they were lifelong friends, but Khama had a cunning that they could never rival. In this instance, their minds raced with ideas about what Khama was really up to. They couldn't be sure, but they knew their safest course was to take as much control of the situation as they could.

"Perhaps Khama's idea is the wisest course. If our city is to be aligned with Egypt, no other kingdom or tribe could say that they were interested in an alliance with us also. But we are well known in these kingdoms, and even my sister has married a man from the Uuma tribe. My king, send me to the tribes so that I may ascertain their thoughts and plans," the first advisor said.

"And I should see the kings. Because of your generosity I have been able to visit with many of them, and I know the advisors very well. I would not bring back to you any disappointment, only the truth of what these kings' thoughts are concerning us," the second advisor declared.

Nospri gave a nod to both men. Then, he looked at Khama. "These men have strong relationships with the other tribes and kingdoms. I trust them to be truthful, and so can you. If you are correct in what you assume about the other kingdoms wanting an alliance, I promise you that we will consider more before any envoy is sent to Egypt."

Now was their chance. They didn't know how they would do it at first, but Azmera and Khama knew that they could make their decision to remove the two advisors work.

The day after the discussion with Nospri, Khama met with Azmera under the pretense of having an interest in her garden. Khama suggested that they truly meet in her garden, but Azmera forbade it, even for this. Instead, they met outside the city walls.

"They will be leaving in two days. We must act fast if we are to gain control," Azmera said.

"It would be too suspicious to have both of them killed or make them disappear. He would certainly suspect me," Khama pleaded.

"And yet, they must both be gone."

"The king is sensitive about betrayal. Let us start there."

Two days later, both advisors left on their missions. Azmera and Khama delayed their attempts to hurt the two men while they were gone. They wanted to see what reports they would bring back first, and they were curious as to what Nospri would do if they brought back favorable reports. Meanwhile, they considered other options.

While he was at the Uumas' small settlement, the first advisor, along with his two accompanying guards, one of which was Bon, wasted no time in finding out the feelings of their tribe. Arriving late in the evening (which was done purposely, for the Uuma thought it a hindrance to deal with outsiders during the time of day when they should be hunting, working, or cooking), the advisor presented the chieftain with a gift, a necklace, that Nospri himself chose for him. The chieftain liked the gift but not the givers. The Uuma preferred isolation from other tribes and kingdoms, and the chieftain wasted no time in letting the advisor know it.

Pleased at the response, the advisor told the two guards that they would not linger long in the land, but head back home in the morning.

The three set up camp outside of the Uumas' land. They ate roasted pig and drank sour wine made from figs that the chieftain reluctantly shared with them because of the necklace gift. Nevertheless, it was a large amount of meat and wine, and as their campfire flickered, the satiated men prepared to sleep. But the advisor was too happy and excited to rest. He constantly got up to walk around, started singing, and even broke out into laughter as the others tried to sleep.

"Why do you laugh and sing?" Bon asked, as if knowing the cause would help put an end to it.

"For vindication! Vindication! I told the king it would be this way, yet he still needed to see it! Well, see! These foolish cockroaches have no desire to be anything but foolish cockroaches. They should be coming to us looking for an alliance, not the other way around."

"An alliance?" the other guard asked. They were not told the nature of the journey, only that they were to protect the advisor.

"Our wise king saw the need to humor Khama by seeing if nearby tribes or kingdoms wanted to ally themselves with us," the drunk advisor revealed to the guards.

Bon and the other guard became concerned.

"Are we considering a battle with another land?" Bon asked.

"No, but we are considering how to make our land grow rich and strong. It is true, we will have to make concessions by allying with Egypt, but they will pale compared to the riches we will receive. The Uuma, the Meroians… the others, we gain nothing from them. We are already stronger and richer than most of them—they would be a hindrance to us."

"Many, yes. But not the Meroians. They are a strong and noble land. Surely an alliance with them would benefit us both, to say nothing of all the tribes that are between our lands," Bon said.

"You sound like Khama, to your shame. To join with Meroe would only bring wasted conflicts and wasted time. Our kings would not agree on most matters and would not trust each other on others. However, to find favor in the richest land… that is where our thoughts should be—to the north!"

"I have heard that they believe we are black because their gods have cursed us. How would they ever be willing to show respect to our land and king? The cursed land. Perhaps they would treat us no better than foolish cockroaches," Bon said as he turned over to try to go back to sleep.

The advisor's blood began to boil. His drunken anger led the advisor to rush to Bon and kick him in his upper back as he lay on the ground. Bon, though he was much bigger and stronger, attempted to control his instincts and not retaliate. This was the king's advisor and good friend; he could not hit him. But since the man was so drunk and barely able to stand, Bon decided to use this against him. He stood up. Now the advisor was swinging punches at Bon, so Bon moved quickly to avoid one of the blows, throwing the man off balance and causing him to land in the fire. This quickly sobered the advisor up and he rolled out of the fire. The other guard, not saying a word, poured water on him and then laid back down. Bon looked over the advisor, who was staring straight up at the stars. He didn't look to be in any pain, although his clothes were still smoldering. Bon thought it would be better for all if he moved his campsite far from the advisor.

Over a hundred miles away, the other advisor was just arriving in Meroe along with his two guards. On their approach to the walled city, they were spotted by a soldier who recognized them from a previous visit that the advisor had made with Nospri months prior. As a result, they were treated extremely hospitably as they walked into the city, almost as if they were royalty themselves. Young children and teenagers ran to greet the men. Women met them with wine and varieties of fruits. When the king of Meroe heard about the visitors, he dispatched guards from his palace to meet the advisor and escort him to the palace.

As he waited for them to arrive, the king frantically directed the servants in his palace to make sure that it was presentable and that the advisor would want for nothing. He instructed his attendants to prepare the best meal for the men who would be dining with him in the evening. The beds that they would sleep on would be made from soft sheep wool soaked in the finest perfume in the land. The king declared that he wanted dancers to entertain them before their evening meal. Finally, he wanted to bestow on him a barrage of gifts to give to King Nospri.

When the advisor reached the king's palace, he instructed his two guards to wait outside. He wanted all his conversations with the king to be private, especially since he was trying to be covert about his true mission. Now, though, based on his welcome, he could tell which way the conversation would lead. Meroe would welcome an alliance, much to his dismay. He quickly tried to strategize how he would change the Meroian king's mind. Changing kings' minds was, after all, his vocation.

The palace was as majestic as the advisor remembered it from his visit months before. Although it was smaller in height than the palaces and temples in Egypt, it still had that same tone- high ceilings, large open spaces and windows, wide pillars that led to the king's throne, which was covered with gold on the arms, but nowhere else. The rest of the throne was made of wood stained crimson. Blood and gold—to symbolize what the king should care for most: his people's lives and prosperity. Contrast this with Nospri's throne, which was also wood but contained no theme.

Rarely, did he ever sit on it because of its lack of comfort, and he gave little concern about giving a chair any meaning.

The advisor followed the custom of the Meroians when he saw the king on his throne, which was to first give a shout of praise for the king. This was followed by praise for the land and the city. Lastly, a request that the king listen to him and give answers when he wished. All of this was done in a singing, melodic tone. When the advisor had finished with all this, the smiling king beckoned him to come closer.

"Please. You are a friend here. Come close and tell me when your king will arrive?" the king asked.

"King Nospri is not traveling here. I have been sent alone by him to speak with you of a matter of importance to him," the advisor replied.

The king was disappointed, but his excitement at the prospect of seeing Nospri was replaced quickly with curiosity as to what he wanted.

"I assume the matter can be discussed after our meal this evening, or is it of greater urgency?"

"After our meal would be an ideal time," the advisor said.

"Then follow my attendant as he shows you where you may wash and refresh before then," the king said as he stood up and walked out of the room, motioning for his six advisors to follow him. The advisor followed the attendant.

Late in the evening, the household gathered for their meal. The king offered the advisor the best of everything he had, and the advisor did not hold back from enjoying it. After the feast was eaten, the king's curiosity could not be contained anymore. He ordered all to leave except for the advisor. When they left the table, the king moved closer to the advisor.

"My threshold for curiosity has been crossed. Tell me why you have come."

"My king loves you and your land. He has always spoken of Meroe as our brothers. But he wants more for his kingdom, and he ponders whether Meroe wants more as well."

"An expansion? Through an alliance? A military alliance?"

"It is only a thought that King Nospri has been considering. It is not a certainty—only a thought."

The king stayed quiet for a moment as he stared at the advisor.

"For such an important 'thought,' I would have assumed that he would talk to me about this himself, not through a servant."

"He did not want to start rumors. On our way here we passed through three tribes that may have become suspicious if they saw King Nospri traveling. Suspicion usually follows a traveling king as people wonder what his plans are. Better that he send me, a servant, to ascertain the feelings of his friend before he suggests any further conversations."

"What more can you tell me about this alliance? Who does he expect would lead this? Has he come to me first?"

"He has come only to you. And without your blessing, I know he would take this matter no further. He would need you if we are to overtake the tribes that pollute the land between us."

The king paused again and gave the advisor a long stare. He had friendly relations with the neighboring tribes and respected them. Since their formation over a hundred years prior, there had never been any altercations between them, only friendly exchanges.

"The tribes are not *pollutants*, nor would they cause any problem were we to ally with one another," he said coldly.

"But surely their chieftains would not want to give up their leadership to follow yours or king Nospri's. That is the true reason why they dwell in between our cities. To ask them to give up their freedom only for an inclusion that they do not desire would not be successful."

"You are speaking Nospri's words?"

"Oh, yes. I advise the king on many heavy matters, and most of these matters spark a long debate. But not this. On this matter, we see the path clearly. The tribes must be conquered or absorbed by our kingdoms."

The king was speechless. The Nospri whom he knew would not suggest a massacre of innocents. However, he began to believe that the advisor was right. The tribes would have to be absorbed, eventually, into their kingdoms' expansion. More people, more land, more tribes—that was the whole point of an alliance. Still, the king was not ready to give a definitive response.

"You have given even me much to consider. And I shall consider this matter deeply over the next set of days. But it has grown late, and now I must lie down. My attendants will make sure that you will have all the gifts that I bestowed on your king when you leave in the morning. You may tell Nospri that I will think on all that you have told me, and I will send my own advisor with my response to him. Soon." The king turned and left the room.

The advisor sat with himself, proud of what he accomplished. He knew that Meroe had good relations with the neighboring tribes and that it would be unthinkable of the king to turn on them. He left the room and went to his soft bed with a feeling of satisfaction. He hoped that his cohort had been successful as well (but not as successful as he).

Days later, when both advisors had returned home, they had another meeting with Nospri and Khama to discuss their options. They went out into the courtyard to speak. Previously, this had been Bon's area to guard, but the first advisor had spoken so badly about him that Nospri felt he had no choice but to move him to the prison.

The fresh sharp morning air that seemed so pure and exciting to Khama went unnoticed by the other three men. As they walked, the first advisor whispered to the second that Khama had been scheming something; no one had seen him for days. They could tell that whatever he had been doing, it affected King Nospri very much, judging by his demeanor.

When they were alone in the courtyard, Nospri raised his open palm to Khama.

"Go ahead. Speak. Tell them what you discovered," Nospri said.

Khama fought back his excitement and tried to show a face of compassion.

"While the two of you traveled west and south, I traveled north. You may remember on our last journey to Egypt, I cultivated a friendship with a man named Fahreemti, the prince of a province south of Cairo. He has grown in power and esteem since we last saw him; he visits the pharaoh frequently. I advised Nospri that it would be good to know, from an Egyptian, what steps we could take to prepare ourselves for an alliance with Egypt. So, I asked Fahreemti, and he told me, and I told the king. But one matter came up that is most unpleasant. Several years ago, in a certain Egyptian province, a young prince got the mind to assassinate a pharaoh by putting poison in his wine. The scheme did not work, and the young prince was killed instead, when his scheme was found out. The pharaoh wanted to know everyone who was involved in the plan and when he found out that the princes' childhood friends were his advisors, he became very angry. To him, this arrangement seemed like nonsense because he believed that a prince's advisors should always be significantly older and that having a contemporary advisor leads to unproductiveness, laziness, and…well, the whole of the matter is this: After having the advisors killed, the pharaoh ruled that no prince or governor or ruler of any kind in Egypt have advisors younger than they were unless they were old men. If we were to pursue this alliance, then both of you would have to be removed from your positions as advisors."

The men waited. They waited to hear what the king was going to say. They wanted to attack Khama but wouldn't dare do so in front of Nospri. So, for a full minute, the four of them stayed silent. Finally, after thinking about the greater good, the king spoke.

"I do not want this. I do not agree with this. But as king…"

"You must do what you think is best for the land. I do understand that," the first advisor said.

"I do as well. King Nospri, it was a privilege to serve you," the second advisor said.

"Hold your tongues. I have made no final decision," the king said as his voice cracked.

"My king, for the alliance to work, you must show them your best. They must not see too many differences between us. Any actions that you could take to make us more similar to them will help the alliance move forward," the second advisor said.

"Yes. With this—our last service to you as advisors—we respectfully remove ourselves from your service," the first advisor chimed. This was not the way dismissal was usually handled, but Nospri was so emotional that he allowed it.

"Leave us!" the king yelled at Khama, who then quickly left the courtyard and went looking for Azmera. The lone advisor left the three of them with a smugness in his heart and pride over what he and Azmera were able to accomplish.

The king hesitantly walked up to his two friends. "I know that Khama schemed this somehow. I want you to be cognizant of my awareness of that. Still, to please the Egyptians…"

"We understand. And we still wish to serve. We cannot do so now, in this land," the second advisor said.

"But we can serve you in others. Permit us, please, with your expressed blessing, to leave for Meroe and Kahfuum. If your alliance with the Egyptians is to work without hindrance, you will need people in these two kingdoms to report to you whether or not they will be any trouble for you," the first advisor said.

"Spies," the king said as a smile broke loose in the corner of his mouth.

"No attempt at an alliance would be successful without them," the first advisor said.

"Who would go where? And when would you report back without being noticed? I do not want even Khama to know about this," the king said.

"I should go to Meroe. It has been years since I have been there, and I do not believe I would be recognized," said the first advisor.

"And I will go to Kahfuum. I do have a friend in the city. We will only reach out to you if a circumstance warrants your attention or warning. If possible, we will try to control matters to the best of our ability. And yes, it is vital that Khama not find out about any of this. He is becoming more cunning... somehow. Despite his smiles, he is still set to destroy any hope of an alliance with Egypt," the second advisor said.

Nospri got the essence of what the advisor was suggesting. He knew Khama was smart, but he didn't believe he had much ambition. At this stage, he knew what the correct step might be, but he was not wise enough to actually take the step, at least not on his own. Nospri knew that Khama had someone pushing him into taking the actions that he did, and he knew who it was. For her part, Azmera had kept up appearances very well, never giving a hint of the plan she had worked out with Khama. Nospri was pleased with how the advisor addressed the subject, giving no disrespect— only an allusion.

"You will be alone with him now. Your only advisor is scheming against you. Who knows how much damage has already been done? In my last act as your advisor, I suggest that you move quickly in your plans and that you keep them to yourself. Decide on when you will see the pharaoh yourself and then leave the next day. As you leave, make sure that Khama or anyone else you have suspicions about stays here and does not travel with you," the second advisor advised.

"If you do not know their dealings, it is vital that they not know yours," the first advisor said and then quickly realized his mistake. He should have said "his dealings," not "theirs." Nospri noticed the inference but let it pass.

"Should I not just have him killed?" Nospri asked.

"No. He apparently has friends in Egypt and has made himself known there. At this time, you can still use him and turn his actions against him the way he did to us. But you do not want the pharaoh to learn that you killed Khama. Then you would have no advisors, and the pharaoh might try to ascertain why and discover that the two of us were your child-hood friends. No, for now, he should live. But when, or just before, based on your judgment, the alliance is made, kill him. Do not banish him. Kill him," the second advisor said.

From the corner of his eye, Nospri saw Azmera walking up to him. She had a young female servant with her who was carrying a platter with fruits and vegetables from Azmera's garden. He turned to the advisors.

"Stay in the land two more days before you leave. We still have much to ponder." The advisors nodded and walked away, the opposite of Azmera's direction. She knew they suspected her of being behind what transpired. She wanted to give them a small sampling from her platter but decided to turn around when she saw the stern grimace on Nospri's face.

The two advisors never returned to the land. They both hoped to be utilized as advisors again, but it never happened. They were able to negotiate positions as governor and ambassador, but only over very small provinces.

CHAPTER TWELVE

A few hours before sunrise, Bon and Kito walked into the prison. Kito had his hands tied behind him as if he were a prisoner being taken to a cell. A bored guard approached them.

"A new prisoner? This late?" the guard said.

"Yes," Bon replied.

The guard slapped Kito in the face and told Bon to give him the worst cell in the prison. When the two men were out of sight of other guards, Bon untied Kito, and the two men walked to Tizzra's cell, removed the stones blocking the entrance, and hurried inside.

"You will have to talk to him hastily. The other guards might come through here soon," Bon said to Kito as he left the cell to keep watch.

"Why do you dwell here? What occurred?" Kito asked as he looked at the lump of dirt where Tizzra just buried his mother.

"Azmera had me and Chara brought here a day ago. She said that Chara had stolen one of the rings that Nospri had given her. Chara is in here too. Have you seen her?" Tizzra asked as he stood up, something he had not done since his mother had been brought to him.

"No. I will see her after I leave you... if no guard catches us. Is your mother also in the prison? I went to see her, but there was no one at your home."

"Azmera killed her. Sidra brought her in here and I buried her right there." Tizzra looked down and pointed at the ground. He turned his head away from Kito.

"She killed your mother over a ring?"

"Sidra stated that Chara may be next. He wants me to help him kill Azmera. I need your assistance, Kito."

"Sidra is your hindrance, Tizzra. He has something to do with all of this. I have heard that Azmera does not know where you are. The guard who let me in here said that when he saw Chara a day ago, Sidra warned him not to let anyone know that she was here," Kito told Tizzra as he glanced back at the dirt covering Tizzra's mother.

"Why would Sidra do something like this to me? Many times, he has told me that I was like a son to him." A statement Sidra never said to Tamrin.

Bon walked back into the cell with a long piece of cloth in his hands. The guards used this type of cloth to cover sick or dead prisoners. He had noticed a lot of his fellow guards discuss going inside the prison because the sky looked as if it was about to storm.

"We need to depart now. I will try to slip you back in here tomorrow," Bon told Kito.

"Tizzra, I will not be able to see Chara tonight, but I will try tomorrow. We have to leave now."

Tizzra wasn't listening much to Kito. Again, he was focused on his mother. Without saying anything else to Tizzra, Kito walked out with Bon and the two men quickly replaced the stones covering Tizzra's cell.

When they were done with that, Bon took the large cloth he was carrying and covered Kito's entire body with it. Then he picked Kito up, tossed him over his shoulder and walked out. Few guards said anything to him. They simply assumed that Bon was carrying a dead prisoner. One hundred feet away from the prison, the same guard that slapped Kito earlier walked up to Bon.

"Is he dead or sick?" The guard asked as he pulled out his blade in case the prisoner was only sick.

"He is dead," Bon replied.

"Do you require help burying him?"

"I will take care of it alone," Bon said as he walked away from the guard.

* * *

Hours later, just after sunrise, Sidra returned to the prison. He tried to avoid as many guards as possible, knowing that the fewer people that saw him, the better. When he approached the stones outside of Tizzra's cell, he noticed that they seemed different than when he last left. Sidra could have become very worried about this, but he wasn't sure of the stones' previous configuration. Regardless, he removed the stones quietly and walked inside.

Tizzra had just gotten to sleep after being awake since he first arrived at the prison. He was lying on the ground with his back turned to the entrance.

"Wake up!" Sidra shouted and then looked around to see if anyone heard him.

Tizzra rolled over. He stood up as fast as he could and focused his mind on where he was. Sidra looked around the room.

"Where is your mother?" Sidra asked.

"I buried her in here."

"You should have yelled for one of the guards. They would have—"

"Evil may have prevented me from protecting her, but Love has allowed me to show respect for her by performing the burial myself," Tizzra interrupted. "And I do not want anyone to try to remove her."

"Focus your anger, for Evil is plotting on killing Chara. But I can fashion a scheme for you to get close to her to kill her. And after it is over, you will not be punished. In fact, most will never know that you had anything to do with it. You see, Khama will be in charge after she is dead. He also holds that she should be removed." Sidra disobeyed Khama's direction that they tell Tizzra to merely overthrow the queen. He wanted her dead.

Tizzra stared at the floor for a moment.

"I do not know if I could bring myself to do it. To be the one responsible for our leader's death," Tizzra said.

"She is responsible for thousands of deaths! And the only way her terror will end is if she is gone! When your blade draws near her, meditate on your mother and your wife and my sons and all our friends who died in battle. Tizzra, this land was in harmony once. We can reestablish it." Whatever Sidra lacked as a general, he made up for in his tirades. As a speaker, he and Khama could talk any soldier into doing virtually anything they wanted them to do. Before the soldiers left for Egypt, Sidra learned that some soldiers were planning on running away. He wanted to discourage this because he knew that Azmera was planning on having any defectors killed along with their families. He also knew that her threat was serious. They had a higher chance of surviving the battle than they did of escaping from Azmera. Tizzra had high respect for Sidra, and until now, he had never questioned his guidance.

Sidra sat down on the ground next to Tizzra and looked at him.

"What do you think our brothers thought about Azmera as they marched to their deaths? Did you imagine any felt honor or love? If they did, I suppose they were the first to die! How could you throw your spear at the Egyptians who never harmed you, but have hesitation for the snake who killed your mother? She challenges us to see our limits, and I hope she has found yours. I pray that killing your mother was a boundary for you, that you will not let her go further and kill your wife also. You spoke about nothing but Chara for days on our journey to Egypt." Sidra referred to Tizzra's fellow warriors as 'brothers' in an attempt to make him feel closer to them. It didn't work. Tizzra only had one brother, and he had left the land years prior.

"Describe what you want me to do," Tizzra demanded.

"Before the next sun rises, I will send Tamrin here to get you. He will accompany you to Azmera. Do not squander time or stamina talking to her guards, for they desired to meet you. I will arrange it so that our men will not be far from her palace. Do not say anything to her and do not let her say anything to you. If she screams and her guards hear her, then all of our plans are destroyed."

Tizzra stared back at Sidra. After a long pause he asked, "That is it?"

Sidra let a grin show. "Yes. That is it. That is all that is needed to bring peace back to our land. That is all you need to do to salvage all of us. And you will be blessed for doing this. I can promise." This was not the plan that Khama told Sidra to tell Tizzra. Again, Khama wanted her alive so she could experience traveling to Egypt knowing that she faced certain death, the same way her warriors did. So he wanted Tizzra to overpower and gag her so she could not scream. Then, he was to signal the other soldiers stationed nearby by throwing a torch out of her window. Sidra knew this was going to cause a significant argument between Khama and him, but it would be a small price to pay to see Azmera gone permanently.

Sidra stood up. Meanwhile, Tizzra dwelled on what was expected of him. Physically, he was capable of the task, he knew that. He resolved to sit in his cell all night and prepare his mind for the assignment. Over and over, he would tell himself, "She killed your mother. She is going to kill your wife." He turned to Sidra.

"Tonight, I will be ready."

* * *

The queen sat on a stool in her newly burgeoning garden, satisfied with the aromas that were penetrating her nostrils. Everything was progressing as it should, she felt, and the imagery of her dead parents pushing the vegetables through the soil after they spent weeks examining it for their daughter gave her a reflective sigh. These sighs, and clear, clean water, were the only things Azmera gave back to her garden. She assigned a servant to take care of the fertilization, insects, and other creatures. This was her temple when she would connect with the land and her ancestors, both of which gave her a good life. There was more spirituality for her in this garden than in any temple she was ever forced to walk in. In her whole life she never voluntarily or unbegrudgingly went into one. As a young girl, the ceremonies and dress of the grown men made her laugh, but as a woman the formalities angered her because she saw them as a tiresome charade. At least, she realized when she was younger, she left the temple with a good laugh she would share with her brothers. But since Nospri died, she hadn't set foot into a temple. None could give her the clarity of thought that her garden did, so why would she muddy the waters? Why would she disrespect the extremely rare gift of connectivity that she was experiencing by walking into a different temple? Her temple was free of walls, rituals, commoners, and apathetic hearts. "Only a pure heart walks into my garden. Not like the many that are forced into the temples." She was forgetting about the servant who cleaned her garden every day, of course. She was apathetic about cleaning out dead leaves and insects.

Indeed! Azmera's garden, though not particularly visually stunning, did grow the best food in the land. Not only were her cucumbers abnormally large; they seemed to experience longevity, lasting days longer, without wilt, than any other in a thousand miles. Her onions grew quicker than the average and no flavor was sacrificed.

Azmera dedicated her garden to what she knew grew the best in the area as opposed to what she desired most to eat. If not for the fact that she believed her garden to be her personal spiritual oasis, she would have offered her produce to all of her servants and guards regularly. But as it was, the yield was not to be wasted on others. When she did occasionally give it out, there was always a motive behind it. To persuade one to do what she desired, usually. Which was another reason she wanted to see Tizzra so desperately. He must be fed from her garden too if her plans were to come to fruition. How she regretted that she didn't feed the entire army before they went into battle, despite giving every general a potato except, ironically, Sidra. Only two of the generals ate them. Selections from her best vegetables went to the king of Meroe when she requested guards from him. The king loved what he tasted and selfishly ate all thirty pounds of it himself in a week. He even raved about the food to Delo before he left their city.

* * *

After leaving the prison, Sidra went to Khama's home. When he got there, he noticed a group of men standing outside of Khama's hut. Khama had been asking different soldiers to find out who would support what they are planning to do. A careless move, but it did work in his favor; none of the men who were approached rejected the idea. Most of the men were soldiers who fought with Sidra in the battle. Others were prison guards, the same ones Sidra was concerned about seeing Tizzra and Chara. The sight of soldiers standing around made Sidra nervous. When he left Tizzra, he started feeling good just like he did before he had heard about Azmera's plan to strike Egypt. However, that feeling disappeared quickly when he saw the soldiers. Sidra did not know that Khama was planning on recruiting so many others in their cabal. He was known throughout the land as someone who was very passionate and blunt, seldom considering the consequences of his actions. In truth, he was not much different than Azmera, except he had a spoonful more morality. Sidra felt that he had gone too far this time by having a large group of soldiers meeting outside of his home, forgetting how this might be perceived by others who lived nearby.

The soldiers were happy to see him. When they noticed him, they approached to greet him, some with smiles on their faces. He pushed past the soldiers and went inside of Khama's home without announcing himself.

There were four more guards inside of Khama's hut, including Bon. They were drinking wine with Khama when Sidra entered. "Khama, I need to talk to you," he said in his most serious tone. He did not notice Bon because his back was to him. Khama left the group and walked out of the hut with Sidra. The two men started walking a little distance away from the soldiers.

"Why are those men standing outside? They will attract attention to you!" Sidra said loudly. Khama was insulted by his tone, but instead of making a scene, he simply turned toward the men.

"Go home! Someone will be by each of your homes later to talk to you more about what we discussed." With little hesitation, the men started walking away, each heading to their hut.

Sidra started to feel a little relieved. Again, though, he started looking around to see if anyone was looking in on them, and again, no one was. Sidra decided to keep the conversation short and direct. "Tizzra will do it. Tamrin will go to the prison tonight and escort him to Azmera's palace. I told him not to talk to her, just subdue her," Sidra said as he turned to walk away. Khama was worried about what might happen if she got the chance to talk to Tizzra. She could persuade him to aid her. He grabbed Sidra's arm to keep him from walking away.

"Tell Tizzra to be at her palace just before sunrise. Azmera usually goes up to the roof of her palace to watch the sunrise. There will not be any guards around to stop him since she does not allow anyone to come up there when she practices this ritual and he can easily get in the back entrance." Khama let go of Sidra's arm.

"I will tell Tamrin to tell Tizzra when he goes there," Sidra said.

"Tamrin is an idiot! I will not have him tarnishing our plans because of his incompetence. I want a guard or soldier to go with him," Khama said. Sidra nodded in agreement. "I will choose the man myself," Khama continued. "He shall meet Tamrin outside of the prison after sundown, and the three of them will go to Azmera's palace and wait there until sunrise. Afterwards, they should all be brought here."

"I understand," Sidra said as he again turned to walk away. Khama went back inside his home. The soldiers had drunk the rest of the wine and were growing impatient, waiting for Khama to tell them his plans.

"I need one of you to accompany Tizzra and Tamrin to Azmera's palace tonight," Khama said to the four guards. Bon instantly volunteered. The other men had drunk much more than him in a spirit of *pre-celebration* and were slow to do nearly anything. Khama liked Bon because of his famous disagreement with the former advisor. He grabbed Bon's arm and led him outside to talk to him.

"I assume that you already know that you are not to tell anybody about this. You should hurry to the prison right after you leave here. Tamrin will be there at sunset, and then the three of you will go to Azmera's palace and wait there until sunrise. Then Tizzra will go into the palace. When Tizzra comes out of the palace, you are to all come back here. That is all you need to know."

Bon nodded his head and started running away from Khama.

From the corner of his eye Khama saw his wife returning home. He had given her instructions that she was not to return until sunset. After the sun had retired for the day, he would tell her not to stay in their home or even the city. He and Sidra had to protect their wives. They debated where they should shelter them to shield them, not only from Azmera and her guards if their plan were to somehow fail, but also to prevent them from knowing the details of their plan. Khama never knew that Sidra had already told his wife about the revenge plot; he would have chastised him for doing so and demanded that Oja be kept close to them.

Khama's wife was not known for her intelligence. In fact, she was viewed as dumb by many in the village, especially Azmera. She was pretty in her youth and fought over by men and these two factors (mainly the second) were the driving force behind Khama wanting her. But through the years, he too grew tired of her lack of concentration and savvy. Azmera encouraged him to take a second wife, but Khama couldn't be bothered. The country, in his mind, was his first wife- the woman was second. He'd give his life with a smile for the first, but the second…

"Why have you returned?" Khama said sternly to the grinning woman. He grabbed her by her arm and pointed to the sky. "Do you not see that the sun is still burning?! That is the sun!"

"I forgot something. Let me get it and I will go again," she said.

"No. You will go now, and you will not speak to anyone for the rest of the day. Yours was the simplest of tasks, and you have failed."

"Why are there so many soldiers in the village? Did you give them a meal? I could have helped. Call them all back and I will prepare something for them."

Khama looked at her for a moment and came to a realization that he had been letting himself ignore. *This woman is to be the new queen? No. She must be hidden. I will have to take another wife.* But this was a problem for the future. For now, he didn't trust her to be out of his sight, so he led her inside the hut and looked around to see if anyone noticed her.

But there was no one in the village. Khama's village was hit very hard by the battle. Many of the generals and their families lived in the same village as Khama, which was by design. The village was located on a steep hill, which would give everyone a good view of any attack coming from the north/ northwest. The generals had a path laid from the village to the palace. There were double the number of rocks surrounding most of the other villages' walls. And just outside of the village were two wells that no one other than the generals, their sons, and Khama were allowed to use. And now, Khama had very few neighbors, all of whom were weeping widows and their daughters, who stayed inside of their homes and mourned. Khama had heard their mourning ever since their men left for

Egypt. He stayed awake at night and listened to their prayers and even became moved to tears when one night some of the women, unplanned, began praying and singing to their ancestors outside of their homes. After a time, they began to sing the same song:

"They were all we needed.

We are so alone.

We want to be there with them.

We are so alone.

Spit on us if it brings us peace.

We are so alone."

Over and over Khama listened to this. They were talking to their ancestors, but Khama took it as though they were addressing him. Such desperation. And it didn't take long before all of the women joined in unison. Khama noticed when each woman joined in. He knew when Heda's wives sang out through their tears. He heard Coasha, the large wife of a general, who would also lose a son in the battle. As Khama lay there safe on his bed, the only man left in the village, he told himself that something must be done. Most of his neighbors would not be coming back to their wives and children. As a neighbor, he must do all that he could to take care of these women. These women were the same ones that Azmera would call weak and unsupportive when Khama went to see her the next morning.

CHAPTER THIRTEEN

The sun was starting to relent. The sky was turning crimson, and the first cool breeze of the day had risen. Insects were forming bands and everything in view had a reddish hue on it as if the land was inside an oven.

Kito was farming with his sons on this evening, gathering the yams that he had planted on land a lengthy walk from his home. Bon had been running since he left Khama's house. Kito saw Bon running up to him, so he sent his children away. He was certain that something bad had happened to Tizzra. Kito walked slowly to Bon because his fear made him feel weak.

"Death tonight! I learned that Tizzra is going to Azmera's palace tonight! I am to take him there, along with Tamrin. And it is graver than we assumed. Khama is involved, too, and so are many guards and soldiers." Bon said all of this between his gasps for air. "I was going to see Azmera herself to tell her about what they are planning, but if I did, they would simply deny it. And if I could not prove it, Azmera would have me killed!"

"Perhaps we could just tell her that they have Tizzra in the prison. She has been asking for him and cannot find him," Kito said.

The two men stood silent as they thought about that idea. "I fear that I may have spoiled that plan by coming here instead of going to the prison. Tamrin will be there after sundown to go with Tizzra and me to the palace. By the time I would get back to the prison, it would be night. When Tamrin sees that I am not there, he will inform Sidra or Khama and they will slaughter Tizzra. They will have to if they want to conceal what they have done, and there are so many with them. But now, let us not squander any more time. If I am not there to meet Tamrin, he will know that something is wrong."

Kito looked back at his home to verify that his children were inside. He stared back at Bon. "Let us go!" he said as he started running. Bon, although very tired, started running after him.

The sun had been gone for some time when Bon approached the prison. Kito didn't come with him; he was hiding between the rocks behind the prison. While Bon was walking up to the entrance, he saw Tamrin coming from the east, carrying a torch. Tamrin noticed Bon, who was covered in sweat, and approached him.

"Are you prepared?" Tamrin asked.

"I am," Bon said as he breathed heavily.

"I am too. This morning I woke up in a pleasing mood! I am very much ready to receive our future! At last, my life will be healthier! I—"

"If you are ready, let us go in," Bon interrupted.

Tamrin walked into the prison, and Bon followed. There were no other guards to be seen. Khama had wanted as few guards around as possible because he was unable to learn whether they all were on his side. To make sure that there would be no trouble with them, he told Sidra to dismiss all of them for the night. Tamrin started talking again while the two of them were removing the large stones that blocked Tizzra's cell. "We are to walk to the palace. While Tizzra is inside, we will go around the back and wait for Tizzra to bring her out to us. She might be dead before we see her." After Tamrin said this, all the boulders were removed, and the two men walked into Tizzra's cell. Tamrin continued, "Khama wanted me to remind you not to let—"

Before Tamrin could finish his sentence, Bon threw him against the wall and beat him until he was unconscious. Tizzra stood back while this was happening. Bon took a rope that he got from Kito, stood Tamrin up, and tied him up.

Afterward, he took a long piece of cloth and placed it in Tamrin's mouth as a gag. "Kito is awaiting us. We are going to take you to Azmera. We will tell her everything," Bon said.

"What about Chara? We have to get her first!" Tizzra demanded.

"We can. But we suspect that she would be safer in here. On our way to the palace, we might run into some of Sidra's men. If they saw a woman traveling with us, it would hint to them that something is wrong. I propose we leave her where she is and enlighten Azmera that your wife is in peril; that way, she can hold off on her punishments until Chara is safe."

"I must at least see her," Tizzra said.

"I would not advise it. To learn what has happened and to know that it is not over yet would only upset her more. And we do not have much time. Let her sleep for now, and when she finally sees you, it will be in a peaceful world," Bon uttered.

Reluctantly, Tizzra agreed. Bon turned back to Tamrin and took his clothes off, rolled them up, and carried them with him as he walked out of the cell. After that, he and Tizzra replaced the boulders.

Tizzra and Bon went over the nearest hill where they met up with Kito, who had just finished rubbing moist sand over his face, arms, hands, and legs in a bold attempt to make his skin look as light as Tamrin's. Kito put on the clothes that Bon took from Tamrin. Now, if any guards saw the three men passing, at least from a distance, they would think that Khama and Sidra's plan was being carried out.

"It will not take long to get to Azmera's palace if we went directly," Kito said, "but we must be careful not to encroach too close to any of Sidra's hidden guards. I submit we take the longer path . There may not be as many guards that way." Kito pointed to the route that he was suggesting. Bon was exhausted and became even more so when he saw the proposed route. Even so, he knew that that was the best course to take. Tizzra paid little attention to where Kito was pointing. He was simply glad to be out of the muggy prison and breathing fresh air. Kito touched Tizzra on the shoulder and pointed to the route that they would take. This path took them around a village and up a large hill that they would have to circle to get to the back of Azmera's palace. They did not carry a torch. Halfway to the palace, they started talking in low voices.

"When we reach the palace, I must turn back," Bon said to the surprise of Tizzra and Kito.

"Go back? Why?" Tizzra asked.

"I had hoped to get my family out of my village before Tamrin got to the prison. Khama threatened to harm them if I failed him. I must get back to them in time. Then I will go to the prison to make sure that your wife is still safe," Bon said as he stared at his feet, carefully making sure that he didn't take any missteps.

"We will request Azmera to hold off on her punishments until our families are safe from Sidra and Khama," Kito said as Azmera's palace finally came into view.

Bon thought about the other guards who had sided with Sidra and Khama. Most of them were friends of his, but he knew what Azmera would do to them when she found out about the betrayal. They would all be dead soon. Bon knew that he was part of the reason for this. Out of the three, he would lose the most. If Kito's plan worked, Bon would lose most of his friends and two leaders that he had admired in the past. If Khama's plan worked, he would now lose his family, two associates, and his own life. He also knew that he couldn't stay in the land after what he was doing because of the hatred he and his family would receive. Even so, he had to decide between not only his friends, but between loyalty to Azmera or Khama. Perhaps if he had questioned his decisions more thoroughly, he would have chosen a different course since he was not very close to Tizzra, and he liked Khama a lot more than Azmera. But he knew that whoever threatened his family the way Sidra did was his enemy, and he couldn't let them get away with it.

There was also the default in his attitude that encouraged Bon to not see things change. No one had ever successfully overthrown a king or queen in their land before, so why should that happen now? As battered as he knew the land to be, he still felt that Azmera should remain queen. He even used the rationale that this attempt at regicide would be an eye-opener to her, and she would realize that things needed to change—that she had gone too far and would treat the men in the city better. His instincts were driving him, not his wisdom.

"Be certain to inform Azmera that *I* had nothing to do with Sidra's ploys. I do not want to encounter any of her guards," Bon pleaded.

"Of course, we will tell her. Are there any other guards that were not in on the plot either?" Tizzra asked.

"In their conversations, they yield to Sidra," Bon said hesitantly.

"That may be because Khama threatened their families like they did yours," Kito replied.

"Yes. That may be correct! Still, Azmera will not credit that."

"Quiet. Get down!" Tizzra told his two friends. The three of them hid behind a row of rocks near the palace. Tizzra pointed to two of Sidra's guards who were hiding behind Azmera's palace.

"Those men are with Sidra. How are we going to get around them?"

Bon ran up to the two guards. His hands were waving frantically, he had a frightened look on his face, and he was limping. The two guards put their hands on Bon's shoulders to calm him down enough to get information out of him.

"He escaped! Tizzra escaped!" Bon said with force but not so loud that Azmera's guards would hear him. He continued, "He cast Tamrin down on a rock when my back was turned. I wrestled with him, but he ran off!"

"He undoubtedly went back to the prison to liberate his wife," one of the guards said as he let go of Bon and started to run in the direction of the prison. "Come, Bon. If we encounter Sidra or Khama on the way, *you* must take blame for what happened."

Bon hesitated. If they went back to the prison, they would find Tamrin there. Still, Bon faked an injured leg and started walking as slowly as the guards would let him. Tizzra and Kito watched all of this with frustration and anxiety because they didn't anticipate Bon would leave them under these circumstances. They would have to meet Azmera alone and work as fast as they could.

Tizzra and Kito walked to the main entrance to the palace. Rethe was standing guard at the entrance. When he saw Tizzra and Kito walk up to him, Rethe pulled out his long sword. They stopped.

"My name is Tizzra. I need to see Azmera. Are you one of her new guards?"

"I am. Azmera has been scanning for you. She wanted us to meet you." Rethe didn't see a general when he looked at Tizzra. He saw a fortunate boy who could fight well.

The two friends followed Rethe inside the palace. Kito quickly began wiping the sand from his face. The three of them walked past Azmera's new guards, who were on the ground playing a game that was very popular in Meroe. The guards stared at the three men, wondering who Tizzra and Khama were. Delo looked at Rethe and showed him his spear. Rethe turned his head away from him, signaling that he didn't need any help guarding the two men. Instead, he nodded his head toward Azmera's bedroom. Delo understood. He got up and walked over to one of the female servants and instructed her to wake Azmera. After a long wait, Azmera emerged from her room, dressed as if she had never lain down.

"Tizzra!" she exclaimed. "Where have you been? I have been asking around for you for days!"

"Sidra had me thrown into the prison two nights ago. He said that you ordered it because my wife stole something from you," Tizzra said.

"I never ordered anything like that! Guards!" As soon as Azmera called for her guards, Tizzra felt a knot in his stomach. "I want Sidra brought to me at once!"

The guards turned and started to run out of the palace. Tizzra turned to them with his hands raised.

"Wait! Stop!" Tizzra yelled to the guards, who instantly did what he said. He turned back to Azmera. "This involves more than just Sidra. There are a lot more entangled in his plan."

Azmera's stomach developed a knot as well. Her worst fear had come true. She was scared to ask who else was involved, but she had to know.

"Then tell me," Azmera demanded.

"Khama... and many of the guards and soldiers," Tizzra said.

"Except Bon. Bon is a prison guard who helped me get Tizzra out of prison. He is bound for the prison. Sidra's guards saw him, and they made him go with them," Kito said.

"Sidra may have more men concealed around your palace. "If they see all your personal guards run out of here, they will know that something is wrong, and my wife is still in the prison!" Tizzra said.

"I understand. Tizzra, you and your friend go out to my courtyard. I will send an attendant to you in a moment." The two men did as she said. Azmera walked up to her guards.

Azmera's guards were ready to serve their new queen. Many of them stood in front of her with their swords and spears already drawn.

"As you have gathered, there was a plot to kill me. I want Sidra and Khama brought to me alive! The other guards who were with them I want dead. Their families too. You will need to locate a prison guard named Bon. He knows the names of the men who are with Sidra and Khama. All of you cannot leave the palace at the same time because of Sidra's spies. Delo... you and Rethe will go to the prison to meet Bon. I also want you to free Tizzra's wife, and Delo, you will escort her back here. Rethe, I want you to go to the middle of the city and wait there for the other guards to meet you. Then, all of you will kill all of Sidra's cohorts. I want them seized by surprise! Many of the soldiers live in the same village. Surround their huts and pierce them through with your spears! Any man who shows restraint with his spear will answer to me!"

"We understand, Azmera," Rethe said as he left the palace. Delo followed. The two of them didn't run out of the palace, though, knowing that would arouse suspicion. Instead, they walked out of the palace casually, as if they were going to get water from a well.

* * *

Even before she became a queen, Azmera always wanted the land to be a strong one, self-sufficient, with vast borders. She dreamed of ziggurats encircling the palace. She wanted them made of the finest bricks, all of equal measure. They didn't need to ascend to the heavens like the pyramids of Giza, but they should be more numerous. A hundred to start, and as the land grew, a thousand. But the palace—it must be grander than the ones in Egypt. From her garden to the front of the courtyard should be as large as five villages and able to contain crowds of many thousands.

She wanted her warriors to be from the biggest men in the land. Smart and effective too, but her main concern was their physical size. She reasoned that seeing a soldier of such impressive size would be the first blow to an enemy, winning a fight without throwing a single spear. And when they would throw spears or swipe with their blades, they would not only hit their target, but there would be no need to attack again. One attack on an enemy would be enough to destroy. The young queen had dreams of marching her soldiers into other kingdoms in times of peace just to remind these kingdoms that she possessed the best men around.

Azmera was satisfied with her palace when she was first married but quickly wanted more as she traveled and saw how other queens lived. She pestered Nospri to give her marble floors like the ones she saw in Egypt. There should also be torches and torch holders in every room and hallway.

The queen didn't see the physical beauty in gold, but she knew its value and respected it for that. She saw much more beauty in jewels and crystals. She loved the bright colors that came from letting sunlight shine through her emeralds. But since the world loved gold, she must have gold too. She would encourage Nospri to make all their gold in the form of jewelry—her jewelry. The king didn't care one way or the other, though his advisors encouraged him to have gold that could not be easily carried away by thieves.

* * *

The walk back to the prison was very quiet for Bon and the two guards. Before tonight, all three of them had been friends, but now, the situation had changed enough to cause a rift between Bon and the two men.

Bon grew more nervous as he saw the prison getting closer. Still pretending to have a bad leg, he leaned on the shoulder of one of his former friends. The men walked up to Chara's cell. Just like Tizzra's, the entrance was blocked by large boulders. The two guards quickly started removing them; Bon didn't touch them at all.

When all the boulders were cleared, the two guards walked inside of Chara's cell. She was lying on the floor, very dirty and hungry. The guards were confused as to where Tizzra could be.

"Behold her. Though dirty and dusty, she still glimmers like a star. Why would Tizzra not come back for his wife?" one of them said.

"Perhaps we got back here before he did. Look at Tizzra's cell! Why are the boulders back in place?" the other, shorter guard asked. "Bon, did you replace the stones after you and Tamrin took Tizzra from his cell?"

"We did. We thought it would be wise," Bon said as he started inching his way out of the prison. The two guards didn't even notice him. Instead, they ran to Tizzra's old cell and started removing the stones. Bon walked outside of the prison.

Outside, Bon looked up at the night sky, an action he always did when he was in trouble because he believed his ancestors would help him. Bon wasn't scared at all about the guards killing him. He was a lot more scared about having to kill them. He knew that he could get them before they injured him, but he was unsure if he could bring himself to kill old friends.

Bon looked out into the distance and saw Delo and Rethe. He could tell that they were not Khama's men because of their many large, bright ostrich feathers, an outfit unique to Meroe. Excited to see them, he started waving to get their attention. The man reasoned that Tizzra and Kito sent them to help him. He desperately wanted them to deal with his old friends instead. They were hundreds of feet away when they saw him waving to them. When they did notice him, they started running in his direction.

As soon as the two guards finished removing the stones, they looked in and saw Tamrin still unconscious and tied up. Instead of going in to untie Tamrin, the men looked behind them and noticed that Bon was gone. They ran out of the prison to look for him.

Bon saw Sidra's men running up behind him. In front of him were Azmera's guards, but they were too far away to fight with Sidra's guard. He would have to do it himself. These guards, however, had no problem with killing Bon. They ran up to him with their swords drawn.

Bon pulled out his sword, and in one stroke, he sliced both men across their chests. Bon didn't strike with enough force to kill the men; he only wanted to slow down their attacks until Azmera's guards could take over. However, a third guard was watching from behind one of the large trees located near the prison. He had been stationed there since Bon and Tamrin met at the prison. Now, he realized he failed in his duty of making sure that there were no problems with Tamrin, Bon, and Tizzra leaving the prison. This third guard didn't attempt to join in the fight. Instead, he ran off so he could tell others what he saw. Rethe and Delo detoured to the third man, knowing that they couldn't let him warn the other conspirators.

Bon would indeed have to fight his old friends.

As both guards ran towards Bon, he threw his sword at one of them and pierced the man through his stomach. The other guard wasn't intimidated by this at all as he continued running. Bon was now without his main weapon, but he still had a small blade on him. He planned on using it on the other guard when he got close enough, but Delo had thrown his spear at the guard, and it struck him in his back. Both guards fell on the grass, still alive and in severe pain. Bon walked up to them and stood over them. He knew that he should put them out of their misery, but he couldn't bring himself to do it.

After Rethe had killed the third guard, he and Delo walked to Bon.

"You are Bon? Tizzra and Kito told us that you knew the names of all the other soldiers who were with Sidra. We require their names," Delo said.

Bon didn't answer at first. He just stood there looking at his two dying friends.

"I know their names. There are thirty-two of them." Bon turned and looked at the third soldier that Delo and Rethe had killed. "Now, there are twenty-nine."

Delo noticed that Bon was fixated on the two dying guards, so he walked up to the one that he pierced and pulled his spear out of him and stuck it in the other guards chest. Bon turned away quickly and started telling them the twenty-nine names.

In truth, however, Bon didn't tell them the names of all the guards with Sidra. He left five people out of his list of names. These were his closest friends.

After he told them twenty-nine names and descriptions of where these men lived, he started to walk off. Then, remembering something, he turned back.

"Inside the prison, there is another man who allied with Sidra and Khama. He might be unconscious, but he is still alive. Do not forget about him. He is in the last cell. The stones are removed from his entrance," Bon said.

"We will extinguish him right now. Do you know where Tizzra's wife is located?" Rethe said.

"The stones from her cell have also been removed. You will see her," Bon said.

"Are you going home now?" Delo asked and then directed a question to Rethe. "Do you think it sound to let him go home? If another guard saw him alone—"

"I must get to my family." Bon ran off.

Rethe and Delo walked inside the prison. Rethe went into Tizzra's previous cell and approached Tamrin, who was now awake and in tears. When he saw Rethe, Tamrin stopped moving. Accepted defeat. He didn't fight back in his last moments, just looked up at his killer and died. Embe, the man in the cell next to Tizzra, was listening to the commotion.

"What is all that noise?! What is going on out there?!" Embe yelled.

Rethe wiped his sword clean and then walked out of the cell. "Go back to sleep! There is nothing going on out here that concerns you!"

They never told Delo her name. If they had done so, Delo would have had time to speculate, hope, and worry. As he stepped over the rocks and into the cell and looked at Chara, he pondered how it was possible to have a nightmare and a blessing at the same time.

Chara's reaction wasn't much different. She never thought she would see Delo again in her life. That is what the King of Meroe told her anyway when he sent her to Nospri and Azmera seven years earlier. Chara had broken the king's rule and heart by not staying exclusive to him and straying into Delo's arms. Not having the stomach to kill her, he repaid her betrayal with his own, sending her as a gift to Nospri. Delo, he would have killed, but he never knew who the soldier that she loved was.

And now, they were again lost in each other's gazes.

"Chara?! You are Tizzra's wife?"

"Why are you here? I heard screaming! Where is Tizzra? What has she done?"

"He is safe."

Chara stared at Delo, then turned her head and ran out of the cell, which she was too terrified to do before. She looked up the hallway to Tizzra's cell and hurried to it. All she saw was a dead Egyptian teenager. Then her eyes found the lump of dirt that was Tizzra's mother's grave.

"Do not fear; that is not your husband. We are to take you to the palace to see Azmera. Your Tizzra is there as well. We must hurry. All will be explained."

It had been several years, and yes, she was now married, but Delo was disappointed by Chara's reaction to him. He attributed it to the trauma she had been through. If she had seen him under more propitious circumstances, he reasoned, she would have shown more delight. On the other hand, he knew he was the cause of so much difficulty in her life. Had she never gotten involved with him, she would still be in Meroe.

CHAPTER FOURTEEN

The death of his mother was the only thing that would make Tizzra turn against his fellow soldiers. He assumed (incorrectly) that they all knew what Sidra and Khama had done to his mother and approved of it. After all he had done for them, saving most of their lives, coddling their fragile egos whenever he received praise and they didn't, spending countless hours with them to help them become better soldiers. And now this. "Did none of them speak out when Sidra made the suggestion? How could they have justified it? This is what they do to a helping hand? Cut off the entire arm?! Their anger over Azmera should not have let them betray me! But I shall certainly let my anger over what they did to my mother betray them. If it can be called 'betrayal.' Let it be called 'revenge,' for I can bear it. If vengeance can engulf this land like a morning mist, who am I to be immune to it? Let me take leave of my senses like the rest of the men. How would it profit me to be the only sane man in a city of jackals? I must match their despicable attitude. Take sadness from my heart and fill it with vengeance; otherwise, I will not know how to move from here to there."

* * *

In Azmera's palace, Tizzra and Kito were sitting in Azmera's court-yard. Kito took advantage of every luxury that Azmera's servants offered. Determined to please his senses, he ate the queen's food, pickings from her garden that she really wanted only Tizzra to eat. The cucumbers seemed

140

to give her comfort when she ate them; perhaps the same could happen to Tizzra.

Kito looked at the beautiful scenery from the courtyard. The last time he was in the palace was the morning after his hand was mauled. On the walk to the palace, he wondered if Azmera would remember him or even the event that led to him losing the use of his hand.

The scenery was beautiful only because it was nighttime and most of the land could not be seen. Had he been there during the day, he would have absorbed the same depression that Azmera's guards had as they looked out on the land. But the night covered so many negatives: the betrayal, the schemes, the sorrowful widows and traumatic orphans. It made the city seem tolerable.

He smelled the ripe fruit and fragrances in the palace. He noticed this scent as soon as he entered. It struck him as peculiar that even at this late hour, the palace was as busy as if it were the middle of the day. The reality was that this happened more than most in the city knew. During the day, Azmera would pull servants and guards off their chores for the most asinine reasons and usually for long periods of time, but she still expected their chores to be done. When she rested at night (or napped during the day), the staff caught up.

The tired man listened to a servant musician and allowed a servant to wash his feet. All of this was done for the benefit of Tizzra, of course. Azmera could care less about a disabled man, even if he did play an integral part in her not being overthrown—he was merely doing his duty as one of her subjects. So even though the last thing she wanted to hear was music, she let the servant play and hoped that it would soothe Tizzra. He must associate the queen with pleasure.

Tizzra, however, didn't drink her wine or eat any of her food. His attention was divided between Chara's wellbeing and Sidra's betrayal. He fought back every urge to run out of the palace and go to the prison. Kito also helped him quiet this urge by assuring him that this was the safest course since Sidra's spies were probably still around. Despite the precautions, he was still nervous about her safety as well as his own. He was smothered by the feeling that danger was all around her.

Azmera wanted to go out to talk to Tizzra but kept finding reasons to avoid it. The queen did hurry to visit her garden. She approached her favorite tree and began pulling fruit off and eating it like she was in a frenzy. Normally, she would indeed have clarity on a situation after doing this, but there would be no placebo effect this time. Eventually, she mustered enough courage to go out to her courtyard. Her right to rule had been challenged, and this bruised her self-respect. But she would again offer some of her fruit to Tizzra in an effort to bond him to her.

"Tizzra. Your reunion with your wife is only moments away. Rethe and Delo are my best guards," Azmera said and sat down next to Tizzra. Kito looked at her hand; she was holding something in her right hand very tightly, but he couldn't see what it was.

"Have you uncovered Sidra and Khama?" Tizzra asked.

"No. But I think I know where snakes hide."

"When your eyes behold them... you are going to kill them?" Kito asked Azmera.

"With boundless joy! Still, I want answers. I want to know who coaxed the other. Tizzra, do you want to know why they injured your mother?"

"They *killed* my mother. And I already know why."

"Your head will always hold the memories of your mother. I know you feel that you will never be happy again, but what is happiness except a bundle of beautiful memories? Her death was unnecessary. I want Sidra to admit to me why he did it."

"Perhaps he became used to unnecessary killings," Tizzra said. He at last reached down and started to eat some of the food that Azmera had set out for him and Kito. Expressing his feelings to Azmera made him feel better. Azmera, however, was as sensitive as an eyeball to any attacks on her judgment.

"And when do you think that Sidra had killed anyone unnecessarily?" Azmera asked.

Tizzra stopped eating. He looked Azmera directly in her eye and asked her what every soldier who fought with him wanted to ask: "What was the reason for the battle with Egypt?

Azmera felt as if Tizzra was indeed betraying her. She wondered how much Sidra and Khama had brainwashed Tizzra. "You were at the assembly I had two days ago. I told everyone there that Egypt has plans to enslave us. I was obligated to protect my people."

Azmera knew that her small kingdom was no match for Egypt's. Most of the men in her land were satisfied being farmers instead of warriors; thus, Egypt's army far outnumbered hers. Even so, Azmera could not just let them walk in her land and take slaves when they wanted. She wanted the Egyptians to know that her people would be uncooperative to anything that the Egyptians had planned, and she wanted them to think that her people would rather die than become slaves. Azmera did not want to be a conquered queen, embarrassed in their hieroglyphics. Let their pictures show that the Nubians were slaughtered, not embarrassed. Let future generations learn that her citizens would drown themselves before they would let Egyptian shackles be put on them. Let everyone know that the Nubians were the greatest civilization that ever existed because they never bent under anyone's whip. This was Azmera's dream.

Azmera stood up and walked out of the room. Kito looked at Tizzra and tried to comprehend why he would talk so honestly to their queen.

"She may chastise you for that," Kito said.

"Possibly. But she needed to hear it. Especially from me."

Kito didn't take the conversation any further.

After Azmera left the two friends in the courtyard, she went up to the roof. From there, she could see Delo and Chara walking inside her palace. Her hand opened and revealed the same jewels that Sidra recovered from Nospri's caravan. As she saw her former servant walking safely into her palace, she tried not to be jealous of the young couple but could not contain her emotions. She dropped the jewels on the roof, walked away from the edge, and began crying. For the first time in her rule, she questioned her ability to lead.

Downstairs, Tizzra and Chara were being reunited. Tizzra repeatedly thanked Delo for bringing her back safely. The female servants wanted to gather around Chara and express their concern to their former associate. Azmera could hear what was going on from the roof. Her guards were questioning each other as to where she was. Azmera wiped the tears from her eyes and walked downstairs.

"Chara, if Delo did not clarify to you everything that has happened, Tizzra will inform you. I would like for the two of you and Kito to linger in the palace for a time. At least until the guards are close to completing their missions." Azmera said as she walked over to her guards. "Delo, did Bon give you all of the guards' names?"

"Yes. There are twenty-nine of them. Rethe memorized fourteen of them, and I memorized fifteen. He told us where all these traitors lived, but I was not able to retain all of it."

"That is not a hindrance. Tell us their names and we will tell you where they live," Tizzra said. Kito stared at his friend with disbelief.

"There are thirteen of you. Two of you will enclose these betrayers' huts and pierce them through with your spears and swords. After you have killed all the men that Delo has remembered, you will meet with Rethe to kill the guards whose names *he* has memorized." The moment Azmera finished saying this, her guards surrounded Tizzra and Delo to hear directions to those they would be killing. "Delo, you will not go with them, I want you and Rethe to find Sidra and Khama for me. Tell Tizzra and the others all the names that you can remember, then take Unfaso with you and go and find Rethe. Have Rethe tell Unfaso all the names that he has remembered, and then Unfaso will report back here quickly so that Tizzra can expose where they live. Is that understood?"

"Yes, Azmera," Delo replied.

"Good. I advise you to focus your pursuit in the small cave that is within viewing distance from the entrance of our city. Sidra and Khama are not likely to be in the village or their homes. I presume that they are hiding somewhere. But to be sure, visit their homes, burn them, and if you should observe only their wives there, kill them and bring their bodies back to me."

Delo walked over to Tizzra, Kito, and the guards and began telling them all the names that he remembered. Tizzra, subsequently, told the guards where Sidra's men lived. The guards worked in pairs, and after they remembered their way to some of the homes, they left the palace. When Delo finished telling the names, he and Unfaso went to meet Rethe.

Tizzra couldn't help feeling raw about innocent women and children being killed, especially since he had just lost his mother because of people who shared the same attitude about killing as Azmera. Three monsters playing with innocents for their politics. The only factor pushing Tizzra to Azmera's side is that her enemies killed his mother.

Tizzra and Kito had agreed to search around Azmera's palace for any of Sidra's helpers. When they searched, they found no one, so they returned to the palace.

* * *

While all of this was happening, there were some soldiers who missed it entirely. Soldiers who became separated from Sidra and the warriors on their way back. There were others who conveniently lost track of the warriors on the way to Egypt. And there were two who deserted the men quietly as they got close to Egypt.

Now, most of them had regrouped, embellished the stories of how they survived or avoided the battle, and constantly debated where they should go now.

"We all have families that are desperate to see us. Some of you did not see the horrific battle like I did. It would be a significant relief to our wives and daughters to know that we did not die like that. That we were not bleeding on the end of an Egyptian sword," the first warrior said.

"And what would they see if we went back? We would end up bleeding at the end of a Nubian spear. In front of our wives and daughters!" a second warrior said.

"It may not be like that. With so many men dead, it would be unwise for her to kill any more. She is not so vindictive. But to be sure, I will go ahead of all of you. I will seek out the general first and ask his wisdom. I will not mention any of you to him or anyone else. But I will return here to this spot in two days to let you know the wise course. And, of course, if I do not return… travel to Meroe," the first warrior said.

The stragglers looked at each other to see if anyone had any objections to this plan.

"Two days may be too long. It would look suspicious if you returned so soon and we lingered about. Can you not come for us later that same day?" said a third warrior.

The first warrior agreed and grabbed his spear as he headed back home. He left behind a total of nine men, four of whom were injured, two severely. Three of the men didn't have a scratch on them and they looked like polished soldiers. They didn't possess Sidra's insight to know that they shouldn't walk back into the land so pristine.

The first warrior was a half day journey from the city, and since he wasn't injured like some of the others, he traveled as quickly as he could. His thoughts were as diverse as the terrain that he ran on. Fear of punishment from the queen overcome by fantasies of seeing his wife and two daughters and then back again when he considered the possibility of Sidra suggesting that he was a coward who intentionally avoided the battle and left his fellow warriors unaided.

* * *

Delo found his friend Rethe very quickly after he left the palace.He told Rethe the order that Azmera had given them, so Rethe told Unfaso the names that he could remember directions to. The guard then hurried back to Azmera's palace.

"Azmera stated that we should explore some of the nearby caves for Sidra and Khama," Delo said.

"When we see them, I will pierce Khama. You can assail Sidra."

"No. We are not allowed to kill them. She craves to see them alive. I do not know who she wants to kill after that. Maybe she will do it herself."

Rethe was relieved. Despite everything he learned that Sidra had done, he still had too much respect for him to kill him.

Delo pointed to a cave that was about three hundred feet away from where they stood. "That is the one. Azmera seems sure that that is where they are."

"We have to examine a cave at night? They will have the advantage of us if they are in that cave."

"I doubt that Sidra is in that cave. If he were, then he could see us right now, and if he could, I think he would run off."

"No, no. You have Azmera's voice. Sidra is no fleeing deer. Evoke the stories our king told us before we came here. I think he is in that cave," Rethe said, tightly gripping his spear as he started running toward the cave. Delo wasted no time in following him.

As Tizzra and Kito spoke to Azmera's guards, Chara went to speak to her former fellow servants. There were nine of them grouped together, speculating about the events taking place. Some of them had tried to eavesdrop on Azmera's conversations with her guards but could only make out a few verbs and nouns without risking getting caught by Azmera. One of them tried to take a platter of fruits to Tizzra and Kito so she could find out what was going on, but Azmera quickly saw her and waved her off. "Sidra," "Bon," "slaughter," and "surround" were the clearest words. And now, for some unknown reason, Chara was in the palace and approaching them.

"Chara, what is happening?"

"There has been an attempt to assassinate the queen. Tizzra discovered it. General Sidra had us thrown in prison to make Tizzra kill the queen, but he got free and told the queen about it," Chara said in a monotone. Partly because she knew most of the servants would not have minded an assassination if it led to their freedom.

"Did he take your ring too?" one of the servants asked, looking at the spot where Chara had worn her ring.

"Yes. Yes, he smashed it after he threw me into a wall," Chara said. She felt that telling them the truth about what she did to the ring would come off as unappreciative.

"Were you beaten?"

Before Chara could respond, Azmera walked into the room.

"Chara, Tizzra is requesting you," the queen said as she looked over her inquisitive servants. Chara left them immediately, and Azmera bent down and picked up a nearby bucket and held it out for any servant to grab. Normally she would have tossed it at them. "The guards have been out following my orders. They will be thirsty and tired when they return. Make sure everyone has his fill of water."

A servant received the bucket and hastened outside to a nearby well.

"My queen, is there anything you desire?" Another servant asked. The queen hesitated.

"No. Only make sure the guards are refreshed," Azmera said as she walked out of the room.

* * *

While Umfaso was returning to Azmera's palace, Tizzra, Chara, and Kito were planning on leaving. Azmera didn't want to spend a lot of time around the three of them, so she had sent servants to encourage them to stay until the guard returned. Kito, however, saw the guard inside of the palace, and he and Tizzra walked to meet him.

"Tell me the names so that we can leave," Tizzra said.

Umfaso wasted no time in doing what Tizzra demanded. After he memorized all the locations that Tizzra said, he left to find his fellow guards. Kito turned to one of Azmera's servants. "Tell Azmera that we have done all that she has asked and that we are leaving now." The servant nodded her head in acknowledgment and ran out of the room.

Tizzra, Chara, and Kito didn't wait for her to return. They walked out of the palace and headed home. Azmera saw them leaving from the palace roof.

"Tizzra!" she yelled. "This palace must see you tomorrow! We have platters full of unsaid words! And I will keep Sidra and Khama breathing until you have returned!" If Azmera hadn't made that promise, Tizzra wouldn't have even considered returning to her palace the next day.

"Then you shall see me tomorrow," Tizzra said as he and his group started walking again. Kito was sure that he could hear some of Sidra's men screaming in the distance. Tizzra and Chara, however, didn't notice anything because they were preoccupied with their own thoughts.

Eventually, the three of them arrived at Tizzra's home. When they got to the outer fence, Tizzra turned to Kito.

"Our future—it is owing to you. Every child that Chara and I have will owe their existence to you as well as us."

"If only Azmera, Sidra, or Khama had a friend with even half of your integrity, they would be a satisfied creature. Their plans would not shatter!" Chara said.

"You have always been a noble friend to me. One should expect no less from a worthy friend," Kito responded.

"Tomorrow, I would like to see you come with me to the prison."

"The prison? Ah...for your mother. Yes, I will join you there in the morning," Kito said as he turned to start his long walk home.

While Kito was walking down the long hill that Tizzra's home rested on, he heard a commotion coming from the direction of Azmera's palace. As he looked over, he saw four men walking into the palace. He strained his eyes to make out who they were, but he couldn't see. Nevertheless, he suspected that it was Sidra and Khama being escorted by Rethe and Delo. Kito thought about going back up to Tizzra's home to tell him that Sidra was caught, but he realized that this was his first night with his wife, so he decided to leave Tizzra alone. Kito rationalized that this would be good for Sidra and Khama too. The longer they went without seeing Tizzra, the longer Azmera would keep them alive.

As Sidra and Khama entered the palace, Azmera screamed at them from her roof. The two men had their hands tied behind their backs; thus, they were unable to defend themselves from the objects that Azmera was throwing at them from above. Even Rethe and Delo were hit by some of her flying objects. They realized that all of them would be safer indoors, so they ran into the palace.

When they were inside, Rethe put his hands on the men's shoulders and gently pushed them to their knees. Azmera ran down the steps and into the entryway where Sidra and Khama kneeled. When she reached the men, she started kicking Khama as hard as she could. After kicking him more than thirty times, she became too tired to start in on Sidra, so she looked at Delo and instructed him to beat Sidra. Delo did so immediately, whereas Rethe would have had hesitations. Azmera gave them a moment to recover after both men were beaten severely. When they did, Azmera began slapping the pair. Tears were in her eyes again, but this time she didn't bother trying to hide them.

"Why, Khama?! Why did you heed this man?! And why did you do it, Sidra? Revenge for your sons? Your stupid, arrogant sons who assumed they would be generals in my land? Listen to those screams, Sidra! For those are the screams of the men who trusted you!"

Khama did not try to come up with any excuse to cover his actions. He decided to tell her the truth.

"This was my design. I was the one who converted Sidra, and I did it because I would not see you as the leader of a barrel of cockroaches. My error was not taking action *before* you sent our soldiers into Egypt. I know you will kill us. But you should also understand that there will continually be men coming after you. These new guards that you have been flaunting will turn on you someday, too, after they ascertain who you really are. And you should tremble because the truth about you, Azmera, is graver than any falsehood that I could ever fabricate! You are a sickle that cuts down wonderful dreams and beautiful beings in the most fruitful time of life!"

"Your wives are dead," Azmera said calmly. "Both of your wives are dead. I had them killed not too long ago. Keep your tears to a minimum because you will soon be with them."

Delo and Rethe looked at each other, wondering if this were true.

If Khama had any emotions about what Azmera had just told him, he certainly didn't let them show. He fought them back, even when Sidra started weeping wildly. Khama wanted to join him, but there was no chance he would do it in front of Azmera.

Rethe interrupted, addressing Azmera, "There are still other traitors. Delo and I will go after them if you do not need us here."

Azmera paused before turning her gaze from Sidra and Khama. When she finally did, she told Rethe, "First, I want you to tie them up in front of the palace. And place torches around them. I want everyone's eyes on them as I starve them to death."

Rethe was angry at himself for capturing Sidra and Khama for Azmera. If Delo hadn't been with him, he would have told Azmera that he couldn't find them. She noticed Rethe's hesitation in tying the men up but didn't make an issue about it. Still, Rethe followed orders in the same manner as Sidra— knowing they might be wrong but obeying anyhow. Delo grabbed Khama and stood him up before he did the same to Sidra.

"Rethe, I will stay with them until you find a rope," Delo said. Rethe walked away to search for rope. He was surprised at his friend's lack of respect for Sidra and Khama. When he returned with the rope, he witnessed Azmera slapping Sidra over and over. Rethe tightened the rope in his hand to control his anger. Delo, knowing that Rethe was having problems doing what he was told to do, walked over to his friend and took the rope from his hand.

"I will do it. I only need you to watch them to make sure that they do not run off." Delo tied their bodies together so that they were back-to-back. Azmera yelled at Rethe to get the torches to put around the two men. As he went to do that, Delo pushed the disgraced men outside of the palace, sat them down in the dirt, and went back inside, where he passed Rethe, who was carrying a long torch in each hand. He went outside and planted them in front of Sidra and Khama. Khama looked up at Rethe. He could tell from the grimace on the guard's face that he had little respect for Azmera. He thought that he would try to reason with him.

"Rethe, this land is sinking. Azmera is slaying the land and her own people! You see it! Do not let her prevail! Untie us! Untie us, or Egypt will sit on all of this land by the next full moon. And after us, then Meroe. I know you esteem Sidra! Do you think he should expire... like this?" Khama pleaded.

Rethe stared back at the palace and then at Sidra. Without saying anything to Khama, he went back inside the palace. Khama sat disappointed for a while and then looked at Sidra. At their capture, Khama repeatedly asked Rethe and Delo whether Tizzra was alive and if he was the one who betrayed them. The soldiers said nothing in response.

"You should have spoken to him. I believe he would have listened more to you, a warrior, than me," Khama said.

Sidra, too involved with his own thoughts, said nothing. He was frustrated. He would much rather have died in battle with the other generals; at least then, he would be respected in the land, and Azmera would've had no one to blame. Sidra's fear was decline; that is, he didn't want to wither like a piece of abandoned fruit. The deaths of the other warriors and soldiers were quick and happened when the warriors were at their best, physically and emotionally. There was no embarrassment involved, no punishment or reprimand, and usually no slow death. Sidra, however, believed that he was cursed. He couldn't bring death to his enemies, but he could bring it to those he loved and respected the most. Death could not come quick enough for Sidra since he had crossed a point in his life where he knew that he would never be happy again. Khama was still hopeful and infected with thoughts of revenge. He continually struggled to get out of the ropes.

"Stop struggling! You are not going anywhere!" Azmera yelled from the roof of her palace. She had been watching the two of them since Rethe took torches outside. Khama looked up at her.

"Azmera! Untie us! What do you imagine the people will do when they see us tied up?! This will not aid you! With us gone, you will maroon your people with nothing!" Khama yelled.

"With our land cleansed of conspirators and traitors, we will triumph!" Azmera walked away from the edge of the roof and went to bed.

Sidra had started crying again. Even though he understood, Khama gave the man no sympathy.

"Why do you persist? Tears will not burn through these ropes," Khama said dryly.

Rethe and Delo ran out of the palace, passing Sidra and Khama.

"Rethe! Untie us!" Khama said sharply. Rethe and Delo stopped running and looked at the two men. Rethe started to walk toward them, but Delo stopped him and pointed his spear at Khama.

"You do not give us orders!" Delo said. He pushed Rethe into running again, and the two men were quickly out of sight. Khama finally comprehended that it was all over for the two of them.

"I am mournful about your wife, Sidra. I thought that we hid them well enough... I would have gotten them out of the land... but I assumed... I do not know how she recovered them. I never told any of the guards or soldiers where I hid them."

"You killed Tizzra's mother for nothing! Dozens of men are dead! We went through all of this only to help Azmera butcher everyone we loved!" These were the first words Sidra had said to Khama since they were caught.

CHAPTER FIFTEEN

Knowing that too much speed would cause concern from Khama's men or Azmera's, Bon moved conservatively to get to his home. He ran when he could, when he thought no eyes were on him. He snaked from hut to hut, scouting around for Khama's men, his former friends. He would have to wait until later to mourn his dead companions. For now, his focus was on saving his family.

When he made it to his hut, he noticed that there was no one around. At that moment, the village was quiet and asleep. He went inside and noticed his wife and two sons also quiet and asleep. He knelt down, lightly shook them, and quieted them when they woke. He had spoken to his wife earlier about all the movements that were going on in the city and how they might get tangled up in them. Entangled indeed! Bon was at the heart of both sides of the conspiracy. And now the 'heart' urged his wife to get up, gather what they could, keep their children silent, and sneak out the village.

Bon would step out first and walk some distance before beckoning his family. This went on and on until they were out of the village. Bon felt relieved and was even able to swallow a couple of breaths of relaxation, but then he saw Azmera's guards in the distance, running toward the village he just left. The new guards didn't know what he looked like, except for Rethe and Delo, and they might mistake him for one of Khama's men.

For the better part of seven hours, Bon had been on his feet, running for most of it. The exhaustion had caught up with him. He needed to rest, especially since he knew they would be leaving the city forever and traveling for days. But where to go? He knew very little about the surrounding lands but he did know that since he helped the Meroian guards fulfill their duties he may find some assistance there. He believed that they could get away from the apocalypse the Egyptians were going to release on Azmera's city if they were safely tucked away in Meroe. They might attack the other Nubian cities as well, but they would think twice about Meroe.

For now, Bon decided to let his family rest near the Idris lake. Had he known the company the lake was keeping recently... Moments after he laid down his head to sleep, he heard light footsteps. He slowly reached for his blade, which was by his waist. He kept his eyes closed and determined by ear which direction the footsteps were coming from. He was seconds away from thrusting his blade when he heard the stranger's voice.

"You are with my husband?"

Bon opened his eyes. It was Oja and Khama's wife. The women looked frazzled, beaten, and as weary as the bottom of Bon's feet. He stood up and addressed the women.

"I am Bon. This is my family," Bon said as he pointed to the sleepy children and his wife.

"Why are you out here?" Khama's wife asked.

"They have failed! Is it not obvious to you? Such stupid men!" Oja stated.

"She speaks true words! They have failed. Azmera has started a hunt for them now. I imagine she is searching for you two as well. We venture to Meroe in the morning. You must come with us if you desire to live."

"I will see Sidra killed first," Oja said. Bon and Khama's wife were beyond surprised.

"Your eyes could bear it? No, you speak with anger, but I know you could not truly endure it," Khama's wife replied.

"Bear it? My eyes would savor it! Endure it? My spirit would rejoice over it. I— we—are soon to lose the men who have damaged our lives for so long."

Bon didn't have much patience for this conversation. *Either come with us or move on,* he thought.

"We are traveling in the morning. Come if you choose," Bon laid back down with his wife.

Oja and Khama's wife looked at each other and then scuttled back behind the tree where they were before.

"Do you believe it is worth your life just to see our men lose theirs?" Khama's wife asked. Oja gave no verbal reply, but the water in her eyes told her reply. "We will go with this family in the morning." Khama's wife laid on the ground and closed her eyes. Oja stayed awake and fumed over not being able to see Sidra killed.

* * *

The Meroean guards had a difficult time convincing themselves to follow the queen's orders. If they had been sure of what their king in Meroe would think of their actions, it would have helped them tremendously. They argued amongst themselves even as they carried out Azmera's bidding that what they were doing wasn't right. Although all of them felt this way to one degree or another, those who were more eager to fulfill their assignment reasoned that what they were doing was no different than going into an enemy land and decimating it. Of course, the order to do so would never come from the ruler of the decimated land, other guards would argue. But one fact remained clear: the king of Meroe sent them to do a service. They were Azmera's property for the time being.

In the middle of the night, many of Azmera's guards had returned to the palace. Blood dripped from their spears and onto the floor. The guards did this intentionally to show Azmera the results of her impulsiveness. Delo and Rethe, however, were still "traitor hunting" in the village. Spirits were dark among Azmera's guards. Walking past Sidra brought the spirits down even lower.

Kito was slow and tired on his journey home. A couple of Azmera's guards slowed him even further when they asked him for more directions to some of the soldiers' homes. On his way home, he was stopped by an elderly man he knew. This old man had a bad habit of persuading young men to help him do work on his farm for nothing in return. Kito was rarely able to be talked into this.

"Kito! Come here," the old man demanded. As Kito walked closer to him, the old man continued, "Find a shelter promptly! There are bizarre movements in the city. Azmera is stirring. Her guards have been attacking people all over the land."

"I have knowledge of it. I expect she will explain everything to everyone tomorrow," Kito said and started to walk off before the man stopped him again.

"You know what is taking place? Then tell me."

Rather than trying to avoid the old man's further pestering, Kito explained to him what the guards were doing.

"Some of the guards and soldiers that were under Sidra and Khama fantasized a revolt. Azmera learned about it and had them killed, along with their families. That is why you heard her guards attacking people. No innocents died tonight."

The old man was not looking at Kito while he was saying this. His eyes were focused on the large hill where Tizzra's home stood. He saw four of Azmera's guards walk up to the hut and surround it.

"Your friend, Tizzra, is that not where he lives?" The old man said, pointing to Tizzra's hut. Kito turned to look. He couldn't believe what he was seeing. He didn't waste a second screaming or yelling at the guards;

instead, he started running to the hill as fast as his tired legs would carry him.

But it was too late. By the time he got to Tizzra's home, the guards were withdrawing their bloody spears from the hut. Kito dropped to his knees and put his face in his hands when he saw this. The guards took no notice of Kito until he did that. Then, believing him to be a relative of the "traitor" they had just murdered, they aimed their spears at him. Rethe told the guards to wait when Kito moved his hands from his face. The moment that Rethe and Delo recognized him, they knew something was wrong.

"This is Tizzra's hut! Tizzra and Chara are in there! Why did you kill them?!" Kito cried with warm tears falling on the dry dirt ground.

Delo, saying nothing, looked at Rethe suspiciously and walked to the front of Tizzra's hut. When he looked inside, he saw both Tizzra and Chara lying dead on the floor. He walked up to Rethe and the other guards.

"You told us this hut belonged to a traitor!" Delo yelled at Rethe.

"That is what I was told! The man in the prison, Embe, he told me that the man who we killed in the prison, the man with the tan skin, lived on this hill!" Rethe said to Delo and then turned to Kito. "The man in the prison, what was his name?"

"Tamrin," Kito answered in a quivering voice.

"Embe told me that he knew where his family lived. He told me that Tamrin's family lived on this hill and that he spoke coarsely about Azmera! And Bon said he was a traitor!"

Embe didn't know Tizzra's name. He only knew where Tizzra lived and that Azmera had killed his mother. After Tamrin was killed, Embe yelled at Rethe that Tamrin's mother was buried in the cell's dirt floor. He gave Rethe directions to where Tamrin (actually, Tizzra) lived. Embe begged Rethe to free him in exchange for the information. Rethe refused but agreed to mention him to Azmera for a lighter sentence. Contrary to what Delo believed, Rethe honestly brought the guards to Tizzra's hut by accident.

For all the courage they possessed, all the deaths they caused and witnessed over the years, neither of the soldiers had the strength to go into the hut. Their attribute of courage blocked other qualities. Of course, it blocked the negative ones such as cowardice and complacency, but it had prevented the admirable qualities of humility and empathy. Nothing could coax those qualities out of the two men even though they knew there was a slim chance that one could still be alive.

Delo slowly pulled out his blade as Kito came close to them, unsure of what he would do after learning of his friend's death. Rethe felt as if a spirit was at work in the land. A cruel one that kills men who yearn for peace. How can such madness exist just a three-day journey from his homeland? Why were he and his men affected so quickly? He reflected that his father used to tell him that there are some spots on land and sea that do not belong to man or beast but to something else. He knew that they must leave as soon as they could, or they would receive the same fate as Tizzra.

Then he pondered if it was already too late. His king in Meroe had told Azmera that he, Delo, and the other guards were now hers. Why did he have to use that term... "hers?" It had only been a day, and they had heard and seen what happened to things that were "hers." How she spit on things that were "hers." How she destroyed things that were "hers" the way a child would to anger a parent.

Must go. Go. This land has sickened us. I must get us all to safety. But the monsters know that I am aware now, and so I must be clever, Rethe thought as he sat on the dirt beside Tizzra's hut. He was too entrenched in his thoughts to register Kito's yells of grief as he held Tizzra. Delo stood erect and looked into the distance, determined to keep a strong face. That crumbled, however, when he heard Kito crying over Chara and yelling her name. Delo put his hands over his wet eyes and hesitantly lowered himself to his knees.

"What kind of land is this?!" Delo yelled.

"Forgive me for not knowing, but we are getting out of it. We must gather the others first. Come," Rethe told Delo as he stood up.

The old man who had been talking to Kito minutes ago ran through the village yelling, "Azmera killed Tizzra! She killed Tizzra!" Waking up to this bad news was too much for the village. Within a matter of minutes, everyone was awake, grieving and angry.

They were tired of Azmera's decisions that led to their friends and families dying. They always hated having a distrustful leader who believed that a trivial disobedience could lead to regicide. And now, just as Tizzra unknowingly contributed to his own death by not accepting Sidra's proposal, Azmera's paranoia had defeated her because most people in the land concluded that Egypt would invade them soon. They needed a general in charge of their land, not Azmera. She had also done herself a disservice by having most of her military killed.

A revolt was in the air; it couldn't have been stopped. Tizzra gave the people hope. He was a role model for young boys, and many older men and women admired his strength and courage. The people grasped that all the young men whom they admired were dead, so they must be the ones to do what they thought was best for their land.

Men grabbed spears. Women grabbed torches. They all ran to the palace. As they got close, they noticed Sidra and Khama tied up.

"Sidra! Sidra, look!" Khama said and tried to stand up.

"Are they coming after us?" Sidra asked.

"I do not know. Get up."

Sidra got on his feet. He could hear his name mentioned by people in the crowd. Khama correctly assumed that they were not after the two of them, but Azmera. "She killed our wives! She had us arrested!" Khama started yelling. Sidra stood silently, still in pain, and surprised at the hundreds of people that he saw carrying torches, spears, and swords.

"She is in there with only a few of her guards! We need her alive! Go and get her!" Khama yelled. Within seconds, the villagers swarmed into the palace. Some looking for Azmera, some for her jewelry.

There were six guards inside the palace when it was stormed (five fled when they saw the large crowd heading toward the palace). Azmera was in her bedroom, having lulled herself to sleep thinking about what she would do to Sidra and Khama in the morning. She was awoken by the sounds of the mob as they broke into her palace. Although she was scared, she looked out of her bedroom to see if her guards were capable of holding the crowd back, which they weren't. Her guards were not killed, though, merely disarmed and tied up like Sidra and Khama. Azmera strained to hear what the mob was saying. She heard statements like: "She had Tizzra killed!" "Egypt is coming!" and most importantly to her, "We need her alive!" That last statement slowed Azmera's heart enough for her to regain her confidence. She walked out of her bedroom and into the main quarters.

Even though Azmera now had no guards to protect her, she still walked straight toward the crowd in a conceited fashion. Believing that the crowd would be in awe of her and her power, she wanted to meet the eyes of the first person who dared to put his hands on her. No one dared.

"What did I hear about Tizzra being dead? He is not dead! Sidra and Khama were going to have him killed, but I shielded him. That is why I have them tied up outside."

But the pair were no longer tied up outside. They were inside the palace, making their way toward her.

"She killed dozens of our warriors at a time when Egypt could attack us any day! She has not been useful to us for some time now. More have died from her breath and lips than from the bows and arrows and chariots in Egypt. Azmera, I offer you the chance to withdraw your power over the land," Khama said in a display to make him look merciful and wise to the crowd. He walked up to Azmera and grabbed her left arm.

"You thought that Sidra embarrassed the land when he was in Egypt? We will see how well you prosper!" Khama said. The mob behind him cheered on hearing this news. Sidra wanted to walk up to her and kill her with one of her guard's blades but that wasn't a possibility now; the crowd would not stand for it. They decided, with their cheers, that Azmera must be taken to Egypt.

While this was happening, Rethe, Delo, and two other guards made their way into the palace. Khama gazed at them for a moment, then walked up to them.

"Azmera is no longer the ruler; I am. She will be sent to Egypt in the morning. If you still feel loyal to her, you may go with her. But if I have your loyalty, you may stay here in our city or return to your homeland. Do I have your loyalty?" Khama asked.

The guards hesitated. Finally, Rethe stepped up to Khama and laid his spear on the ground. The other guards did the same, except Delo. He pulled out his spear and stood by Azmera.

"What do you think you are doing?! Tizzra is dead because of this woman!" Rethe yelled to his friend.

"Tizzra and Chara are dead because of those two. And us. What more do you need to see until you realize that we cannot trust them?" Delo responded.

"If you stay with her, you will die! They will kill her in Egypt!" Rethe said.

"He has made his decision. We need men to escort them both to Egypt!" Khama said. Almost immediately, ten men volunteered, including Rethe. But Khama didn't trust Rethe enough to let him accompany Azmera and Delo. Choosing a faulty escort could prove detrimental; Tamrin proved that.

The only emotion Azmera felt was embarrassment. She didn't care about her fate as much as she did the village seeing her reduced to this position. She feared a decline just as much as Sidra did. She glanced over at the general, who had been quiet during all of this. At that moment she felt anger that her downfall would be worse than the one she had planned for him. She thought nothing about Tizzra, and neither did Khama. Sidra's thoughts were still on his wife and sons and the blame he shared in their deaths.

The women became the most vicious when Azmera was being dethroned. Many of them threw torches down to burn her palace, but the men quickly put the fires out and tried to control the women. Her servants grabbed torches and ran out to Azmera's garden and set it on fire. They pawed at their queen and began to rip her clothes off. The crowd cheered Oja's two friends as they slapped Azmera repeatedly.

A couple of Azmera's servants did feel some grief for the dethroned woman. They had been with her for so long that some form of attachment was natural. Added to their despair was Chara's death. A friend they were laughing with only a few hours prior, who they thought had been saved from her enemies, was now gone. They were losing everything and gaining nothing. As some of them struck Azmera, they did so not only because of her treatment of them, but because she failed to keep Chara and Tizzra safe. For years, she would occasionally yell in their ears or throw water on them or hit them with what she considered soft cloths. In doing all of these things, Azmera thought she was showing kindness to the servants, believing that most of the men in the land would treat them much worse.

The youngest servant, only twelve years old, was too scared to do anything but stand in the corner watching. The oldest servant, who was ten years older than Azmera but still received the same horrible treatment as if she were the youngest, struck the hardest. In any other palace in Nubia, she would have been treated much better and even revered for her knowledge and wisdom in training new servants and keeping the palace running. But Azmera had held her back and refused to send her to another kingdom as a trade. She saw nothing special about an old servant, but now, she was surprised the old lady could hit so hard.

* * *

What phenomenon made the smoke look so green? What did she put on the ground to make her vegetables grow? Khama pondered this as he watched Azmera's garden go up in flames. He didn't want her to see the green smoke and feel that she was correct in believing she was consuming her ancestors, that there was a supernatural element going on, so he told her former servants to take her and get her dressed. They did so, shoving her into her bedroom. Khama turned back to the garden. The green smoke signaled to him that he should slow things down, get organized, restore order. If he thought there was anything special about Azmera's garden, he would have left it untouched, no matter what the mob demanded. The time for anger was done; now it was time to think. Would offering their queen be enough for the Egyptians? What more could they give? Perhaps since they did not lose much in the battle, they would take pity on these Nubians.

After collecting himself and listening to his former soldiers and the guards, Sidra walked up to Khama.

"What burns?" Sidra asked.

"Azmera's garden."

"Why is the smoke blue?"

"You see blue? I only see green."

"Where is she? Dead?"

"Alive. Her servant girls are getting her ready. She must be sent to Egypt as soon as possible."

"I sent men to find our wives. Rethe admitted that Azmera was lying. They still breathe!"

"Is it so," an uninterested Khama retorted. "My wife will enjoy living here."

"Tizzra betrayed us."

"And he paid the price of betrayal. Anything he wanted I would have seen that he got."

"He must have learned what we did to his mother."

"Possibly. We will never know."

"He also had help in his escape."

"General. Let it end here. We are a damaged city, ravaged by revenge. Azmera's and ours. The land can take no more. When that woman leaves this city, she will carry any thought of revenge with her. No more spilled blood." Khama would later feel pride in himself for saying these words to Sidra. He would view it as his first wise decree. With these words, he put an end to the wave of revenge that engulfed the city. The threat or hope of revenge was entrenched in the lives of every adult, and Khama realized that it would probably be in the heart of every child who lost their father in Egypt as well. But he, for his part, must try to put an end to it by stressing forgiveness. Besides that, revenge was just a tool.

The general lowered his head. As he looked at the ground, he realized that he had a connection to the loss of Pnogi's family. Four deaths, all because of his actions or lack of. The thought of being cursed ran through Sidra. He brought death to his own family as well. In all the deaths, he could find some way of justifying his actions. An accident. Following the queen's orders. Following Khama's suggestions. For a brief moment, he wished he and Khama were still tied up outside the palace. But then he shook that feeling off.

"When our wives are here, I shall inform you."

While Sidra spoke this, the servants pushed Azmera out of her bedroom and onto the palace floor. There were much fewer people in the palace, Khama's few remaining men having pushed them outside. Khama looked at the dethroned queen with disappointment. She looked like a servant's servant. Her dirty clothes were ripped and bloodied. They appeared to be loincloths, five or six of them, tied together.

"No. Unthinkable. She must look like a queen," Khama said as he looked around the palace for Azmera's clothes and jewelry. "Go out in the crowd and bring back anything that belongs to her. The Egyptians will see a queen, not a vagrant. That is what we will present to them. Any less would be an insult to them."

The guards went outside and searched the crowd for Azmera's possessions. The servants took Azmera back inside and began to clean her up and put whatever jewelry of hers they could find on her. Khama walked into the room to watch their progress.

On a platter next to Azmera's bed were fruits from Azmera's garden. Khama noticed the platter and told the servants to leave him alone with the former queen.

"Tell me the secrets of your garden. I cannot stop thinking of it. What was its purpose? Why did you let your servants know and not me?"

Azmera said nothing. Khama picked up a piece of fruit and offered it to her. She snatched it and flung it across the room. Khama smiled.

* * *

While the palace was in chaos, Kito was still on top of the hill at Tizzra's home. He had finished burying Chara but couldn't bring himself to bury Tizzra. The grief-stricken friend told himself he would get Tizzra's mother tomorrow and bury her with the rest of the family. While he was digging the grave, thoughts of revenge started to pollute him just as they had infected everyone in the village. Tizzra's and Chara's deaths needed to be avenged! What kind of friend would let someone get away with what happened? Kito decided not to let those who did this to Tizzra get away with it. So, in an effort to give his friend one last accommodation, he decided to get revenge.

The thought of vengeance helped Kito to finish burying Tizzra. While he blanketed him with dirt, Kito started recalling everyone who had a hand in Tizzra's death. There was Sidra, of course, and Khama and Azmera. But it was the guards who carried out the actual killing. Kito would have to kill them too.

When he finished burying the newly joined couple, Kito went inside of Tizzra's hut to grab his sword and spear. Under other circumstances, he would have buried them with Tizzra, but he wanted them for the tasks that he felt were necessary. It should be Tizzra's blade that cut into Sidra and Khama.

In time, Kito walked to the crowd that was surrounding the palace. A dangerous move for him since nearly all the guards who once supported Azmera now supported Khama and could easily identify Kito as an ally of Azmera. Kito listened to some of the talk being spread by some of the crowd.

"They are taking her to Egypt tonight!" one man said.

"She will be escorted by ten strong men," an elderly woman said.

"They are taking her now!" another woman said.

Just then, Azmera's former guards walked out of the palace and cleared a path for the ten escorts. As she walked through her former subjects, all she heard was joy over the fact that she was dethroned. Kito liked that too, but he didn't like the thought of her dying by any other means than Tizzra's spear or knife.

Kito walked close to the guards. He thought that he would kill the first one who said that he was with Azmera. They did indeed recognize him, yet none of them said anything. He got close to the escorts and was a little confused to see Delo being treated in the same manner as Azmera. Nevertheless, he pulled out Tizzra's sword slowly, without drawing attention, and prepared to lunge at Azmera.

But he stopped. Azmera wasn't as guilty as Sidra and Khama were. Those two should be attacked first. And anyway, if he did it out in the open, he wouldn't be able to get revenge on all who were involved. Kito realized how pointless revenge would be on anyone in the land since they would all soon be slaves in Egypt.

And at that moment, the man who had the most reasons for revenge dropped his friend's spear and sword to the ground.

This isn't what Tizzra wanted. He only wanted peace!

He turned away from the crowd, leaving them to fume in their own vengeance, and began his long walk home. The following morning Kito returned to the prison to retrieve Tizzra's mother. While he expected resistance from guards, there was none. The prison had been abandoned. The few prisoners left were forced to find their own escape. Kito moved Tamrin's body out of the way and began digging for Tizzra's mother. He would re-bury her with Tizzra and Chara later in the day. And in a moment of kindness that shocked even himself, he buried Tamrin in the woman's old grave. A sense of peace rushed through him.

No sooner had he felt this than it was disrupted by Embe's pleadings. The prisoner had heard Kito's movements. Kito looked around the cell and the hallway for something to kill Embe with but found nothing. *It's just as well. Without any guards, he will die of thirst in another day or two.* Instead, he just carried Tizzra's mother out of the prison over his right shoulder, her body wrapped up tightly to contain the odor.

* * *

It was in the midst of the chaotic night that the "straggler warrior' returned to the city. Naturally, he went to his own home first and looked for his wife and daughters, but there were very few left in the village. He became alarmed as he saw blood coming from the ground of his neighbor's hut. Then he noticed the holes in the straw hut, caused by the guards' spears. The scent in the air reminded him of the aroma that came after one of the city's bonfires. The scent came from Azmera's burnt garden. The warrior did notice the smoke as he entered the city but cared only about seeing his family. As he walked around his empty village, the eeriness became almost unbearable; he was close to running out of the village but wanted answers first. The smell of Azmera's garden competed with the smell of the dead in the huts. But the lack of sound from anyone in the village was unlike anything he had experienced before. Even the insects that normally chirped seemed to have abandoned the village. He pondered what happened. Had the Egyptians retaliated already? If so, why were the huts not all burned? He realized that the city must hold the answers.

As he approached the city, he saw some familiar faces from his village and felt relief that some of his friends were alive. He asked around until he was able to find his wife and daughters, who then told him of everything that had transpired while he was gone. As his other friends came up to him they each gave a different story of what happened. Some told him that Tizzra died after he attacked the queen. Another told him that the queen's guards were attacking the city based on orders given by the king of Meroe. Still, another told him that Tizzra was still alive and one of the prison guards was watching over him.

Eventually, he mustered the courage to meet up with one of the warriors whom he traveled into battle with. He mentioned the other stragglers and questioned if it were safe for them to return. He was advised to ask Sidra himself about the matter. Since the land was now suffering a deficit of men, they needed all whom they could find.

The warrior walked up to Sidra, expecting him to be angry. However, Sidra hadn't made the connection that the warrior had been missing the entire time. After a brief pause, Sidra finally addressed him.

"What is the concern? Have you no assignment?" Sidra asked.

"I have only just returned. I have heard so many rumors of what has occurred. There are a few others who were injured who are outside the city. They wanted to wait and receive your wisdom before returning."

"You may go to them and tell them they are to return at once. There is much for all to do, and every man has tripled in value due to the queen—due to Azmera's actions. Khama and I will have assignments for everyone in the morning."

The warrior turned away from the newly restored general. He was too elated from seeing his family to leave them again so immediately. He would return to the stragglers in the morning.